MOON HUNTED

Mirror Lake Wolves - Book Two

JENNIFER SNYDER

MOON HUNTED
MIRROR LAKE WOLVES – BOOK TWO

Editing by H. Danielle Crabtree

Author Note:
This is a work of fiction. The characters and events in this book are fictitious. Any similarity to real persons, living or dead, is coincidental and not intended by the author. The author acknowledges the trademarked status and trademark owners of various products referenced in this work of fiction, which have been used without permission. The publication/use of these trademarks is not authorized, associated with, or sponsored by the trademark owners.

ISBN-13: 978-1978473768
ISBN-10: 1978473761

PREFACE

The air around me warmed; the old wolf magick coming to the surface. It blew across my skin, ruffling my hair and sending it flying from my bun. A smile spread across my face as I lifted my arms high above my head. Strands of hair tickled my nose, but I ignored them. Instead, I waited for my wolf to come to me. When a chill slipped along my spine and goose bumps sprouted across my bare skin I knew the goddess of the moon was near. Her magick danced through the air, calling to the wolf inside me. My wolf howled softly in response to her. It was a beautiful noise.

Lightness and loving warmth ignited through my veins as the change intensified. The sensations spread throughout me until an overall sense of weightlessness became all I could feel.

I was air. I was light as a feather. I was free.

Pure love flooded my mind as the cold touch of the Moon Goddess disappeared from my spine to be replaced by an embrace from my wolf. Warmth and the sensation of being grounded and one with the earth trickled through my extremities.

We were one, my wolf and I.

1

I narrowed my eyes at the brown and black fluff ball Gracie held in her arms. He was cute, but I knew he would be a pain in my ass. I prayed Gran would tell Gracie she couldn't keep the puppy.

"Please. I promise I'll take care of him. You won't even know he's here," Gracie insisted.

The dullness of Gran's eyes brightened as she continued to stare at the little fellow. Shit. She was giving in.

"I'll do extra chores," Gracie promised as an added bonus. It was something I knew she wouldn't follow through with. She never did. Gran had to know this too.

"Where did you get him?" I asked, hoping to pause Gran's thought process. My hand fisted around the grocery list she'd given me earlier. "And, who's paying for him? You don't have the money to buy a puppy."

The little guy was a Yorkie. I knew those puppies didn't run cheap. Not if they were a purebred with papers. There was no way my little sister could afford one on her own.

"It doesn't matter where he came from. What matters is that he needs a home," Gracie snapped at me before shifting her gaze back to Gran. "Can we keep him?"

Gran placed a hand on her hip. I tried to read her face but her expression was unreadable. "He's going to be a lot of work."

"I can handle it," Gracie insisted.

This wasn't heading anywhere good. I needed to find a new angle.

"What about his food and shots? How are you going to come up with the money for those?" It was a logical question. One Gran couldn't ignore.

We weren't the wealthiest of people. In fact, money was always a sore subject in our house.

"He won't eat much. He's tiny. And, I'll figure it out," Gracie grumbled making it clear she didn't want me to be a part of the conversation.

Regardless of what she wanted, I had a right to insert myself. I lived here too.

"Mina does have a point. *If* I let you keep him, he'll be your responsibility. That means you're going to have to figure out how to come up with the money to get his shots and pay for his food," Gran said.

Great. It was a done deal.

I didn't hate dogs, or animals for that matter, I just didn't want my stuff peed on, pooped on, or chewed up. Wasn't that all puppies did the first year or three?

I smoothed a hand over my face and tried to contain myself. Why did my little sister always get what she wanted?

"I'll use the money I have saved from birthdays for his shots," Gracie insisted, clutching the puppy closer to her chest. "His food won't be expensive and I'm sure it'll last him a while. I can find ways to earn enough money to keep him fed."

"You'd have to because I won't buy food for him. I won't clean up after him either," Gran insisted. "I mean it when I say he's yours and yours alone."

It was a lie. I knew it was the second the words came out of Gran's mouth. She'd buy food if he needed it, because she wouldn't be able to watch him starve. She'd clean up after him from time to time and she'd help take care of him. She'd expect me to do the same. While it might come off as though the fluff ball was Gracie's responsibility there would come a point where he would phase into being everyone's. That's how it always was with any of Gracie's pets.

"So, I get to keep him?" Gracie's face lit up, making her look younger than her thirteen years.

The corners of my lips twitched upward at the sight of her smile. Seeing her happy was almost worth what I knew I was about to endure with the little beast. Almost.

"I don't see why not," Gran insisted sealing the deal.

Happy squeals echoed through the living room of our trailer. Gracie jumped up and down, shaking the entire structure while clutching her new puppy to her chest. Once she calmed down, she kissed Gran on the cheek and headed to our shared room at the end of the hall, whispering to her new pet as she walked.

My lips pinched together as I fought to hold back the string of swear words building across my tongue. I'd cursed in front of Gran before but she made it known it wasn't something she liked.

I couldn't keep my mouth shut though, no matter how hard I tried.

"I don't want that thing on my bed, Gracie! And he better not chew up any of my stuff!" I shouted after her. "Or shit in our room! I don't want to smell dog crap every time I walk in!"

Gran cleared her throat. My gaze drifted to her. I waited for her to scold me for cursing in her presence. "First of all, language. Second, have faith in her, Mina."

"Sorry. I'll try." I exhaled a long breath, then grabbed my wallet and keys from the kitchen counter. I relaxed my grip on the grocery list I held and took a step toward the front door. Never had I been so eager to head to the store. I needed to chill. I knew I did. Gracie getting a puppy wasn't the end of the world. I wasn't sure why it bothered me so much. "I'm heading out to get the stuff on your list."

"Ask Gracie if she wants you to pick up puppy food before you leave," Gran insisted.

I fought the desire to roll my eyes. Wasn't that something she was supposed to get all on her own? My blood simmered through my veins.

"He'll most likely get hungry once he settles down later and I refuse to feed him scraps. It a horrible habit to start out with."

"Don't we have a bag somewhere from the last time she brought home a stray dog?"

Gracie was always bringing home animals, but puppies seemed to be her favorite. I'd lost count as to how many she'd brought home over the years.

"I gave it away," Gran said with a shake of her head. "Didn't think I'd agree to let her keep another one."

"I don't know why you did," I muttered as I started down the hall.

"I heard that," Gran snapped.

I didn't apologize.

Gracie was sprawled across her bed when I stepped into the room, the puppy tucked up against her side. He was curled into a ball, sleeping. It was cute but not cute enough.

All I could do was stare at its round belly and think about worms festering inside. Its furry ear twitched in its sleep and images of it being flea infested crept through my mind.

Gross.

"I'm leaving for the store. Gran gave me a list earlier," I said as I leaned against the doorframe. "Give me some money. I'll pick up a bag of dog food while I'm out."

Gracie slipped out of bed without speaking and stepped to her dresser. She swiped her piggy bank up and opened the bottom. The puppy wiggled around, adjusting itself into a tighter ball.

"Here." Gracie held out a twenty.

"Okay." I plucked it from her fingers and crammed it into my front pocket. "What kind of food should I get?"

"Any for small breed puppies, duh."

My teeth ground together as I stared at her. She was really pushing her luck with me today.

I pushed myself off the wall and started back down the hall.

"Be back in a bit," I called to Gran once I reached the front door.

Sticky heat rolled over me the instant I stepped foot outside, but anything was better than being indoors with my bratty little sister who always managed to get her way. I tugged my driver side door open and tossed my wallet and cell into the passenger seat before climbing in. The engine sputtered a few times before catching but this was nothing new. My beater of a car had definitely seen better days. Either my dad needed to carve out some sober time to fix it at the next full moon or he needed to fork over some of his beer money to pay for repairs. The money I made from babysitting Felicia's twins wasn't going to be enough.

I rolled my windows down all the way and backed out of our tiny gravel driveway. I headed toward the main entrance of Mirror Lake Trailer Park, but was forced to pause when a navy-blue truck turned into the park. My heart skipped a beat because I knew exactly who the owner of the truck was.

Eli lifted his fingers in a typical male wave as he crept to where I'd stopped. A wide smile graced his perfect lips, one that sent butterflies flapping through my stomach. When his truck window was flush with mine he stopped. My stomach somersaulted as I waited for what he might say. We hadn't spoken much since he'd kissed me the other night. I'd done everything in my power to avoid him during the celebratory potluck meal and every second thereafter.

Until now.

Stupid Universe. It never did let me stay away from him for long.

"Hey." The sound of his voice coerced all of my nerve endings to life in an instant. His arm muscles flexed and bulged as he moved quickly to manually roll his window down further. "Where you headed to?"

"Um...the grocery store," I said as my gaze drifted across his broad shoulders, up his neck, and focused on his mouth that begged to be kissed. Everything I'd felt around Eli before becoming Moon Kissed, before he'd kissed me, had intensified tenfold in the last few days.

"Fun. Want to swing by my place when you get back?" he asked.

My mouth grew dry. "What for?"

If there was news on Glenn I'd be more than happy to stop by but not for anything else. I couldn't. The things I felt for Eli were too hard to ignore now.

In fact, they scared me now more than they ever did.

A beautiful smile stretched across his face. "I bought a gallon of paint and would love help painting my bedroom."

His bedroom? That was one room I should never allow myself to be alone with him in. Sweet Jesus, my body began to overheat at just the thought of what might happen.

"I can't." The words came out too fast and flustered. I cleared my throat. "I have plans with Alec tonight."

Eli's bright green eyes flashed at the mention of his name. Ever since we learned Alec's friend Shane and his older brothers were responsible for the disappearance of two pack members Eli had been leerier than usual of me hanging around him. While I understood where he was coming from, Eli still needed to realize Alec wasn't Shane.

"Will Shane be there?" he asked. His voice had become rigid and there was a vein beginning to bulge along the side of his neck.

"I think so. It's supposed to be a double date. Well, more like a triple date really," I rambled even though I knew Eli could care less about how many people were joining me and Alec tonight. Still, I couldn't shut up. "Benji started dating someone. We're all supposed to hang out at Rosemary's Diner tonight." My lips clamped shut. I'd already given him too many details. Knowing

Eli, he'd show up to make sure nothing happened to me. If he couldn't make it personally, he'd send one of his brothers. Especially if I slipped up and gave him the time we were meeting.

"Promise me you'll be careful." His eyes darkened as they locked with mine.

I licked my lips. "I'm always careful."

Tension rippled from him. He wasn't satisfied with my answer, but he also knew better than to push his luck.

"Right. Listen, if you get bored or your night doesn't pan out the way you thought it would, you know you can always swing by my place and help paint." He winked. A tense smile twisted at the corners of his lips. He was trying to let go of whatever unease learning I'd be in Shane's presence tonight had caused. "It's been a while since our last painting party."

Heat crept up my neck at the memory of Eli pressing against my backside while attaching his phone to the set of speakers plugged into the wall where I'd been painting.

It seemed like forever ago.

"I'll be sure to remember that," I said as I let my foot off the brake and inched my car forward. "And if I learn anything new tonight that might help with finding Glenn I'll let you know."

"Good." The muscles in his jaw clenched tight. "Speaking of, we should set a time this week to discuss the next step in our plan to find him. Especially since scoping out that vet office where his oldest brother works was such a bust."

I pressed my foot against the break, coming to a stop again. "Yeah, wish we could have gotten inside to look around."

It had been stupid going to the place after it was closed anyway. I wasn't sure what we'd thought we'd find. All we'd done was make the animals go crazy.

"We need to find a way to get inside, one that doesn't come off as suspicious. I thought about getting a dog just to have a legitimate reason," Eli chuckled.

"You might not have to. Gracie brought home a puppy."

Eli arched a brow. He knew how many pets Gracie had brought home over the years. "And Gran let her keep it?"

"Yup." I didn't want to get into it. It would only irritate me again.

"Okay, well maybe this is a good thing. I mean, the timing couldn't be better."

My lips twisted into a frown. Although I hated to admit it, Gracie's puppy might be our saving grace.

"True. I could offer to drive Gracie and her puppy to the vet when the time comes for its next set of shots. I can sneak around while I'm there. See if anything catches my eye. We already know there aren't many employees. Shane's oldest brother, Peter, plus three staff members."

Eli shook his head. "No. I don't like the idea of you doing all the dirty work by yourself."

"Do you have a better idea? One that doesn't scream weirdo?" It would seem strange to both Gracie and Gran if Eli suddenly offered to take Gracie's puppy to the vet.

"And you offering to give Gracie a ride to the vet won't? Everyone knows how much you detest animals."

"I do not detest animals. I just don't like dogs. Or cats. Or..." I was starting to see his point. "Okay, maybe I'm a fish person. Fish don't make a mess. They don't chew up shoes or claw you like a monster from underneath the couch when you walk by."

The last cat Gracie brought home did that to me one too many times. It always managed to scare the shit out of me. I was glad she'd found a home for it with someone else at school.

"My point exactly. Your gran is going to know you're up to something if you volunteer."

Sylvie Hess pulled up behind Eli in her tan minivan. She smiled and waved but I knew she wanted Eli and me to get out of her way. There was something in her eyes that said it all. A kid crying from somewhere inside her van found its way to my ears.

"Whatever. Let's talk about it later." I eased my foot off the brake again, allowing my car to roll forward. I didn't want to keep Sylvie waiting.

"Yeah. Don't forget, swing by my place and help paint if your night is too dull." Eli winked before gassing it.

While I waited for Sylvie to turn into the park, my mind raced with different scenarios of how I could offer to drive the little fur ball to his next vet appointment. It seemed like the only way we were getting inside the place. Well, short of breaking and entering. I wasn't sure we would find anything that might pertain to Glenn there, but a girl could hope.

2

By the time I made it to Rosemary's Diner it was after five thirty. I scanned the place half expecting to find Lilly hanging all over Alec somewhere while she took his drink order but she wasn't anywhere in sight. I tucked my long hair behind my ear and started toward where Alec sat at a table with his friends. My gaze drifted from one waitress to another as I walked. Lilly didn't seem to be working tonight, which was a relief. She wasn't someone I tolerated easy. It seemed like whenever I met Alec here and she was working, she blatantly flirted with him in front of me. While he didn't seem to pick up on it, I did, and it pushed my damn buttons. Hard.

Some girls were real pieces of work.

"Hey." I waved as I neared their table, heading toward an open chair beside Alec. It was strange not sitting at the bar. Generally, that was where Alec could be found. At least the sweet tea in front of him was the same. "It's weird to see you eating at a table," I said to him as I sat.

"There weren't enough open stools at the bar," Becca answered for him. "This place is packed tonight."

"All the old people here for the summer from Florida," Benji said.

I glanced over my shoulder at the bar. Elderly people did occupy the majority of the stools. There was one seat open at the end of the bar. Definitely not enough for the six of us.

Speaking of six...

We were missing someone, and it wasn't Shane.

"I thought you were bringing a date tonight, Benji," I said with a smile. Out of Alec's guy friends, he was my favorite. Benji was funny, sweet, and way more accepting of me than Shane—for obvious reasons. "What happened?"

"She'll be here," Benji said as he took a sip from his sweet tea.

He seemed nervous, which I found adorable. Add that to the collared shirt he wore, which I figured was probably from the church clothes section of his closet, and I wanted to reach across the table and pinch his chubby cheeks. Generally, Benji was a dirty blue jeans and plain cotton tee type of guy. I imagined when he stood up his jeans would be free of dirt and he'd have on his good pair of boots. Not the ones always caked in mud.

"We haven't decided if Benji's girl is imaginary or real yet," Shane teased. His eyes didn't shift to me, even though his words seemed directed my way when he spoke. Ever since I'd become Moon Kissed his intolerance of me had seemed to intensify.

Could he feel the change in me since the last full moon?

"Don't give me that crap," Benji grumbled. "You know

she's real. Hell, y'all probably had a class or two with her this past year."

I wondered who she was. Why hadn't I thought to ask Alec what her name was when he mentioned a triple date with her and Benji? At the thought of him, Alec's hand found my thigh beneath the table. He gave it a gentle squeeze, gaining my attention. I leaned toward him and pecked his cheek in a featherlight kiss. It was a simple gesture, but I didn't miss the smirk cutting across his face from it.

"Hey," he said. His deep brown eyes lit up as he flashed me a beautiful smile.

It had been too long since we'd hung out. I knew it was my fault, I'd blown him off so many times the last few days, and now that I was in his presence I regretted having done so. Alec was a great guy.

I returned his smile with one of my own. "Hey, yourself."

"I ordered you a water with lemon." His thumb made small circles along the smooth skin of my thigh. Tiny pulses of electricity jolted through my core at the feel of his touch.

"Thanks." I reached for the glass. My eyes drifted to Shane for whatever reason. He stared at my hand, zeroing in on something that seemed to surprise him. I knew what he saw.

The ring Eli had given me.

The silver ring with a tiny crescent moon soldered to the band. Part of me thought I should hide it, but a larger part argued there was no point. He'd already seen it. It was too late now.

Shane's gaze traveled to the bracelet my dad and Gran had given me next. My heart beat triple time as his gaze turned cold. If that wasn't enough proof to confirm whatever theories he might have had about me, I wasn't sure what more he'd need.

The tiny hairs on the back of my neck stood on end as Shane's gaze lifted to lock with mine.

"Interesting jewelry you have there," he said.

I kept my gaze on him, refusing to look away. Now was definitely not the time to show signs of unease. I needed to appear strong. Sure of myself. Lethal if screwed with. "Thanks. They were both gifts."

"Oh, really?" Shane's head tipped to the side as a wry smirk stretched across his face. Alec and Benji started talking about something besides me, but I tuned them out anticipating what question would spur from Shane's lips next. "What for?"

And there it was. Shane arched a brow as though challenging me to speak the truth about my silver jewelry.

How much did he know about my kind? Obviously, his knowledge was more than I felt comfortable with. There weren't many who knew werewolves existed let alone of our need to wear silver.

"Beautiful. I really like the ring," Becca blurted out. I could have kissed her I was so damn happy for the interruption.

"Thanks," I said as I averted my eyes from Shane to lock with hers.

"I've always had a fascination with the moon." Becca grinned. "It's so beautiful and mysterious."

I opened my mouth to agree with her but noticed a girl with dark curls bouncing around her shoulders walking toward us. She pushed her glasses up on her nose when she noticed me watching her and her cheeks tinted pink as though she was embarrassed to be seen.

"She's here," Benji muttered as he straightened his back and eyed her. Immediately, he became hypnotized by the sight of her.

"Hi, everyone. Sorry I'm late. I had to help my aunt with something." The girl's blue eyes shifted around the table as her thin lips twisted into a friendly smile.

I remembered seeing her around school. She was new.

"You're good. We haven't ordered yet. Mina just got here, too." Benji pointed to me.

Her shoulders relaxed. "Cool."

Benji stood and pulled the chair beside him out for her. "Guys, this is Ridley. You probably remember her from school. She moved here from Pennsylvania a few months back."

"I remember seeing you around," I said while trying to think of what else I knew about her.

"Me too," Alec insisted. "You're related to the Caraway's, right? The ones who own the inn."

"Yeah. That's my aunt," Ridley said as she adjusted her glasses again while situating herself in the chair beside Benji.

My guard went up at the mention of the Caraway family. While I didn't know them on a personal level, I knew they weren't typical residents of Mirror Lake.

The women were witches.

Gran had told me once they descended from a strong line of old magick. It was their magick that helped my pack keep our full moon rituals hidden from prying eyes. In return, we made sure vampires who weren't part of the Montevallo family stayed out of Mirror Lake.

"People say that inn is haunted," Shane said. I shouldn't have been surprised by his bold words or the level of suspicion ringing through them, but I was.

There was something about Shane that always had him reverting back to the supernatural.

"People say a lot of things," Benji grumbled, making it clear he didn't like where the conversation was headed.

"True." Shane shifted his attention to me, spearing me with a pointed gaze. "Doesn't mean they're wrong, though."

A chill swept up my spine but I still managed to keep my eyes glued to his.

"How are you liking Mirror Lake so far? Has the heat gotten to yet?" Becca asked. Again, she'd cut the tension away when it was about to come to a head. "I'm sure your summers were mild in Pennsylvania, at least compared to this."

"You have no idea," Ridley laughed. "We had hot summers in Pennsylvania, but it was nothing compared to this. I'm surprised I haven't melted yet."

"You'll get used to it," Becca insisted before taking a sip from her water. "Did you live in a big city there?"

"Sort of. It was a little bigger than this, but not by much."

"What made you move to Mirror Lake?" Shane asked. His eyes were glued to her in a way I'd seen before. It was the same cautions and skeptical way he always looked at me.

Ridley blinked and the smile on her face began to disappear, giving the impression whatever reason she had for moving here wasn't one she cared to talk about.

"Um...family stuff." She tucked a few curls behind her ear and met Shane's gaze.

Our waitress came to ask Ridley what she wanted to drink and see if we were ready to place an order. Benji insisted on getting an order of fried pickles. He said it was a Rosemary's Diner must. We placed an order for some and asked for a few more minutes to glance over the menu. I didn't need any more time, though. I knew what I wanted. My usual—a cheeseburger and fries. I set my menu on top of Alec's and glanced at Ridley.

What type of magick did she have?

I studied her while she glanced over the menu. No inkling of the magick inside her called to me. Although, maybe that wasn't something I could do. One would think becoming Moon Kissed would allow me to feel things—if other supernaturals were nearby, what magick they harbored if any. I got nothing, though. Especially when I looked at her.

Maybe Ridley Caraway had no magick.

3

By the time our food came, I was starving and the conversation had shifted back to Ridley's aunt's inn.

"How many rooms does the place have?" Alec asked. "I've always wondered. It looks massive on the outside."

"Ten. Well fourteen if you count my aunt's room, mine, and my two cousins' bedrooms," Ridley said before she popped a French fry in her mouth. She acted as though living in such a large house was no big deal. It was to me, though. I'd never lived anywhere besides Mirror Lake Trailer Park. I wasn't complaining, but still.

"Have you searched the place for secret passages since you moved in?" Benji asked. Childlike wonder hung in his words.

"Actually, that's the first thing I did." Ridley laughed. "I was so disappointed when I didn't find any."

"Not even one?" Becca asked. "I figured with a house that big and old there would be at least one."

"I know," Ridley nodded. "But sadly I didn't find anything."

"Maybe you have to say magic words before one will appear," Shane suggested. His eyes drilled into Ridley. I knew exactly what he was trying to do—make her squirm. It was the same thing he'd done when he first met me.

I glanced at Ridley, gauging her reaction to what he'd said. Either she thought he was joking or she was used to people tossing her magick related curve balls.

"Jesus, would you give it up," Benji insisted. He rolled his eyes as he blew out a long breath. "You're the biggest supernatural freak I've ever met. I swear, the old geezers in town feed off idiots like you when they spout all that supernatural mumbo jumbo. When are you gonna realize it's all gossip? Lies and gossip."

"I wouldn't be so sure about that," Shane muttered under his breath. His face flushed, but I didn't think it was from embarrassment, as he picked up his burger to take a bite.

"I don't mind, he's not the first to mention magic to me. Probably won't be the last either," Ridley surprised me by saying. She reached for her water and took a sip. "I doubt there are any magic words that would make a passage appear. If there are, I don't know them. Let me cut to the chase since I can already see where your mind is going." Her eyes focused on Shane as she pushed her glasses up. He held her stare. "No, my family are not Satanists. No, we don't make sacrifices at midnight. No, I can't hex you. And no, I can't make the pimple on the right side of your nose disappear any faster than your current zit cream." She pointed to a nasty pimple on Shane's nose I hadn't noticed until now.

I burst into a fit of laughter at her bold words.

"Burn!" Benji shouted. "That was badass." He shifted to face her. It was clear from the glossy sheen to his eyes and the slight quirk of his lips that whatever he'd felt for her seconds ago had just amplified times ten.

"Yeah," I agreed. "That was pretty good."

Ridley wasn't as shy and quiet as I'd thought. She had more backbone and spunk than she appeared to. I liked that about her. However, it also made me think she might be hiding something else—like her magick.

Would she tell me if I asked her privately? Or should I add her to my ever-growing list of places and people to scope out?

"Anyway," Ridley said. "I've been here a few months and still haven't figured out what you all do for fun." She took a bite of her grilled chicken wrap.

Maybe I could ask Eli about her. He would know more about the Caraway witches and their magick than I did. After all, he was the Alpha's son.

"There isn't a whole lot to do in this town," Alec insisted as he wiped his mouth on a napkin. He was being quiet tonight. Observant. Maybe I needed to make more of an effort to chat with him. Find out if he was okay. "Most of the time we hang here or go to my uncle's property. We built a dirt track there to ride our four-wheelers on."

"That sounds cool," Ridley said.

"Or we go to the movies," Becca added.

"Sometimes we hang out at the lake, too," Shane surprised me by chiming in. "It's a nice place to cool off in the summer. The water is always decent to swim in this time of year."

"There's fishing and camping, too," Benji said. "Anything you can think of that's outdoors really."

"Nice," Ridley grinned. "I love being outdoors, but I've never been camping."

"Seriously?" Benji asked. He leaned closer to her and bumped her elbow with his. An adorable smirk twisted the corners of his lips that had me struggling to suppress an *awe.* "Sounds like we might have to rectify that one sometime soon. Camping is great."

"I'm down for that," Alec insisted. "It's been too long since I've spent a night in the woods. If everyone has the time, we should go this weekend."

An empty feeling settled in the pit of my stomach. Camping in the woods right now was one of the last things I wanted to do.

Shane's eyes were on me. I could feel them. He was gauging my reaction to Alec's suggestion. I couldn't let him think I was afraid to go into the woods. I refused to give him even an inkling.

"Which night?" I asked Alec while completely ignoring Shane.

"Depends on which one you're free."

"Friday or Saturday works for me," I said. "But I don't think Sunday will."

I didn't have anything exceptionally wolfy going on Sunday, but it was still pack related. I needed to help Gran harvest the next bushel of salvia. Even though there wasn't anyone waiting to be Moon Kissed the plant still needed to be harvested. If not it would overrun her garden. Harvesting on a schedule also kept the plant healthy and strong, which increased its potency.

I might not know much about gardening, but I at least knew that much.

"All right, how about Friday night then?" Alec asked. He popped another French fry in his mouth and glanced around the table. "Anyone have to work or already have plans?"

"I've got a job to do with my dad in the city but I should be done before dinner on Friday night," Benji said. "What about you?" He nudged Ridley with his elbow again.

"I have a couple of rooms I'm supposed to clean at the inn, but that's it. It shouldn't take long."

"Okay, the four of us are on board. What about you two?" Alec asked Shane and Becca.

"I don't have anything planned. My boss only has me on the schedule three days next week," Becca said.

She had a job? How did I not know this?

"I didn't realize you worked," I said.

"Yeah, I've been working at the tax office in town for almost two years answering phones and stuff. My uncle owns the place," she said. "I like it, but I don't think accounting or bookkeeping is something I want to do indefinitely. Which is why I'm off to culinary school in fall."

College. I'd forgotten Becca was going away in the fall. It would suck when she left. She was the only girl I'd ever been able to tolerate long enough to become friends with.

I doubted I'd have many more chances in the future either. I wasn't going anywhere. Mirror Lake was my home. My family was here. My pack was here. It was where I would stay. I'd accepted this a long time ago.

Community college was about as far away from home as I was going to get.

"Friday works for me too," Shane said. He didn't seem

thrilled to be reminded Becca was leaving in the fall either. I tried to remember where he'd said he was going to school, but couldn't.

Maybe it was because I didn't give a crap where he went. All I cared about was that he wasn't stay in Mirror Lake. Having his brothers around town was bad enough. Hopefully Shane left and never came back.

"All right, I guess it's settled then," Alec said as he reached for his sweet tea. "Friday night we're going camping."

"I'm excited!" Ridley gushed as she pushed her glasses up higher on her nose. She squeezed Benji's arm and I couldn't help but think they were the cutest couple I'd ever seen.

Shane coughed, drawing my attention to him. His eyes bored into me, causing goose bumps to prickle across my skin. The tiny flickers of enthusiasm I'd felt when it came to spending the night beneath the stars evaporated as I held his gaze.

Oh shit. What the hell had I been thinking when I agreed to spend the night in the woods with Shane?

4

My old beater of a car flew down the dirt road as I headed toward Betty Sue's place. I was on autopilot, only able to think about how my night camping would be. I hoped Shane didn't try anything. I hoped his brothers didn't either. Camping with Alec would be fun. So would spending time with Becca and Benji. Heck, even hanging out with Ridley sounded like a blast, but not Shane. He was not a friend of mine. He was quite possibly not a friend to Ridley either. The guy seemed to have issues with all supernaturals, not just werewolves.

At least with Ridley there, I wouldn't be singled out by Shane.

Even if she didn't have magick like the other women in her family, she still was tainted by it in Shane's eyes. The whole guilty by association rule seemed to always apply when it came to him.

My car thumped over a section of potholes I hadn't remembered being there the last time I drove out to Betty

Sue's to pick up my dad. The last few rains must have washed out the gravel road. I wondered how long it would be before Hershel fixed it.

While I wouldn't hold my breath waiting, considering he was as much of an alcoholic as my father, I knew he'd get around to it eventually. For someone in his sixties he managed to get around well—when he wasn't drinking to escape his demons with my dad that is.

Hershel's pain was all mental, unlike my dad's. This didn't mean they had nothing in common besides their need for alcohol. They also shared the agony of missing their wives.

The difference was, Hershel's wife hadn't left him the way my mom had left my dad, she'd passed away.

Mrs. Ammons had battled diabetes and a multitude of other health issues her entire life. Mildred Ammons was the sweetest woman, though. In fact, she was the only human I ever thought would be worth Changing if it were possible. She deserved to be healthy and happy. Unfortunately, becoming a werewolf wasn't something you could force on anyone. It didn't happen with a bite or scratch like in books and movies. You were either born with the werewolf gene or you weren't. Simple as that.

An old memory of the first time I wished I could change Mrs. Ammons flickered through my mind, bringing with it a smile. I was little, maybe eight years old at the time. Dad had brought me with him to help Hershel fix their vehicle. Mrs. Ammons was sick that day. So sick I thought she was dying. Hershel swore she wasn't. He said she was feeling under the weather was all. I remember being in the living room, doodling on a piece of notebook paper when I heard her coughing. I crafted a plan that would make Dad bring me back the next day so I could sneak her a mug of salvia tea. I knew how becoming Moon Kissed worked even at eight years old. Sort of.

I never got a chance to bring Mrs. Ammons any tea.

Gran busted me snipping leaves off her plant and scolded me harder than she ever had. The image of her crouched down at eye level with me while she shook her finger in my face would forever be burned in my memory. So would her telling me I could've killed Mrs. Ammons by giving her the tea. Apparently, drinking the herb wasn't something humans could tolerate well. Especially not ill humans.

I tapped my brakes, managing to slow down before hitting the tiny bridge barely big enough for one vehicle. Betty Sue's place was just around the next corner. I could picture the white farmhouse before I even saw it. It used to be so beautiful. Nowadays it looked rundown. Since Mrs. Ammons passed the place had seemed to slowly die as though it grieved her loss along with the family. Hershel was too old to properly upkeep the place and I didn't blame Betty Sue either. She did the best she could between taking care of her dad and working a full-time job. Adding in the house was too much. And all the land. There had to be ten acres surrounding the place. I imagined by the time Betty Sue got home from pulling a twelve-hour shift at the hospital the last thing she wanted to do was yardwork or fix things in desperate need of repair on the place.

The white house with green shutters and trim to match came in to view. Its paint was chipped in places, the porch looked unsafe, and two of the gutters along the front of the roof sagged due to built-up debris clogging its inside. None of this surprised me. The place had looked the same for years.

What did surprise me was the for-sale sign to the far right of the property.

Was Betty Sue selling the place? I couldn't imagine Hershel wanting to move out of the house he'd shared so many memories with his late wife in, but maybe Betty Sue felt it was time they moved on. Or maybe she wasn't selling the house, but instead a good portion of the land. Even though it wasn't my business, I knew I'd be asking.

Dad and Hershel sat in the weathered wooden rockers that took up the front porch when I pulled in behind Dad's truck. I turned my car off and robust laughter from the two old men made its way to my ears. My dad was always such a happy drunk. Sure, sometimes he mumbled things about Mom and how much he missed her, but for the most part he was happy.

It was the only silver lining to his alcoholism.

"Mina, what are you doing here?" Dad asked as I climbed out of my car. His words slurred together but I'd long ago learned to decipher what he was saying regardless of how much he'd drank. "Shouldn't you be in school?"

"Graduation was a couple weeks ago, Dad. Remember? I did the whole cap and gown thing?" I started toward the uneven stairs of the porch. They bowed in the center and there were a few nails coming up in places. "Gran cried. You complained you could barely see me because you guys were in the nosebleed section of the auditorium. Gracie said she couldn't wait until she graduated."

"You tellin' me you don't remember goin' to your own daughter's graduation?" Hershel asked. His wrinkled face scrunched together even more as he gawked at my dad. Anger flared through his words. I knew him well enough to know it wasn't all for show. Hershel was pissed. Family meant everything to him. "You ought to be ashamed of yourself. This is your little girl and that was her special day."

Dad waved Hershel's words away. "Ah, hell. I remember going to her graduation. I was kidding, old man."

Whether he was telling the truth didn't matter. Dad had been there. In my memories, he'd been proud and happy, slightly drunk, but proud and happy. That was all I cared about.

"I'm here to pick you up. Betty Sue called and wanted me to come get you," I said as I climbed the last step to the porch. Dad flashed me a look that let me know he wasn't ready to leave yet. I crammed my hands into the back pockets of my shorts already knowing this wasn't going to be easy. "Are you ready? I think they have someplace to be."

"Someplace to be?" Dad laughed. His head tipped back with the force of it as it rumbled from somewhere deep in his belly. "Hershel ain't got no place to be."

"The hell I don't," Hershel insisted. It wasn't clear to me if Hershel actually knew where he was going, or if he just didn't like the fact someone said he had no place to be.

"What's going on out here?" Betty Sue asked as she came to the screen door and peered out. Her face lit up when she spotted me. The smile that stretched across her face reminded me of her mom. "Hey, darlin'. You sure did get out here fast."

"I wasn't doing anything." I shrugged. "Just sitting around."

"A pretty girl like you shouldn't be sitting around on a

Friday afternoon. That boyfriend of yours working today or something?" She cracked open the screen door and motioned for me to step inside.

I'd forgotten the last time I was here I'd mentioned Alec to her. My heart skipped a beat as I waited for my dad to say something about me having a boyfriend. While he knew about Alec and me sort of dating, he didn't like it.

When he seemed to have not heard Betty Sue I answered her while stepping inside the house.

"Yeah, he got a summer job at the feed store stocking shelves." I followed her to the kitchen, leaving our dads on the porch with their cooler of beer between them.

"Have you got a job yet?" Betty Sue glanced over her shoulder at me. There was no judgment in her eyes, which I found refreshing. For whatever reason, the moment someone turned eighteen in this town everyone automatically thought they needed to buck up and get a job or else they ran the risk of being labeled a slacker. It didn't seem to matter if they were going off to college in the fall. Once you graduated you were an adult through and through.

I wasn't sure if I'd fallen prey to the label yet but knew I was inching closer every jobless day I spent in this town.

"No." I shook my head. "You know how Gran feels about me working while in school."

"Oh, yeah. That's right. So, you decided you're going to college then?"

We stepped into the tiny kitchen. The familiar yellow cabinets and white tile countertops put me at ease. I'd spent so many days here when I was younger before Mrs. Ammons passed away it was almost like a second home. Nothing had changed. The tan linoleum and off-white walls still seemed so bland to me. All of the appliances were old, but from the savory scent coming from the oven I knew they were still functional.

I stepped to one of the vinyl covered chairs at the dining room table tucked against a wall.

"The decision wasn't mine. Gran would keel over and die of a heart attack if I told her I didn't want to go to college in the fall. We compromised, though. I get to take the summer off and start in the fall instead of diving right in after graduation like she wanted."

"That's what I did. It's the smartest way to go about it. I had friends who opted to take a year off before starting college. It didn't work out. They never went back to school." Betty Sue stepped to the oven and switched on the light before peering inside. "Where did you say you were going?"

"Just Mirror Lake Community College," I wasn't sure why I'd said it the way I did, as though it wasn't as important as if I planned to attend a University or somewhere out of state. College was college, wasn't it?

"That's nice. I started at the MLCC, too. Got any idea what you want to go for?" I watched her as she pulled a pair of oven mitts from a nearby drawer and put them on before removing a large pot from the oven. The heavy scent of basil and garlic floated to my nose, causing my mouth to water.

"I'm not sure. I'll probably opt to get the general stuff out of the way first and then hopefully by the time I'm finished I'll know what I want to do with the rest of my life."

"You'll figure it out," she said as she set the pot on the stove and closed the oven. "You have plenty of time."

I smiled as I tucked a stray strand of hair behind my ear. "So, what made you decide to visit your sister?"

I'd been surprised when she called earlier asking if I'd come pick up Dad so her and Hershel could get on the road to her sister's place.

Margaret was three years younger than Betty Sue. If you put the two of them side by side you'd never be able to guess only three years separated them. Betty Sue's life had been harder than Margaret's. It made her appear decades older because of it.

Margaret had gotten to go to college outside of Mirror Lake and start her life elsewhere. She hadn't been forced to stay like Betty Sue.

Which was exactly what I wanted for Gracie.

While I wanted her to become Moon Kissed, it didn't mean I wanted her to settle in Mirror Lake like I planned to. I wanted her to explore the world. I didn't want her to think she had to be with our pack until the day she died. She could join another pack or do like so many others and become a rogue wolf, free to roam and do as she pleased without a pack tying her down.

I couldn't do those things.

I was Betty Sue. Destined to stay in Mirror Lake and care for my alcoholic father until he passed away. Gran wouldn't be around much longer, which meant taking care of Dad would be something I'd have to do on my own. I knew this. I accepted it. It was why I always came whenever anyone called saying he was wasted. I'd long ago accepted my role.

"Well, you know how it is. Time keeps ticking away no matter how much I don't want it to. Dad isn't getting any younger. Neither am I. It's been almost seven years since Margaret came for a visit. I figured it was our turn to head her way. I'd like to see my nieces and nephews, too. Have some family time. Some time away from here." She busied herself with cutting up the meat she'd been roasting in the oven, but from the tone of her voice, I knew she was on the verge of breaking down.

Sadness for her hit me square in the gut. Did she feel bad for not visiting Margaret in so long? Or was it that she felt bad because she desperately wanted a break from dealing with everything on her own?

"I hope you have a good time. You'll have to tell Margaret I said hi."

"Thanks. I will," Betty Sue said as she pulled a plate down from a cabinet and began filling it with potatoes, carrots, and a few slices of the meat she'd cut up. "Are you hungry? There's more than enough if you want to stay and eat."

"I'm good, but thanks." It was barely one o'clock. Why was she serving dinner already?

"I know it's early to be eating such a hearty meal, but I wanted to get something decent in Dad's stomach before we got on the road. I learned the last time I took him to his cardiologist appointment in the city it's best for him to travel on a full stomach. He gets crabby otherwise. Plus, he'll generally take a nap for a few hours."

"Sounds like you've got him figured out." I stood and started toward the front of the house to get my dad. "Have a safe, fun trip. I hope he sleeps like a baby for you the entire way."

"Thank you, darlin'," Betty Sue said as she set the plate she'd made on the counter and followed after me.

We walked to the porch. Halfway there I remembered the sign out front.

"I noticed your for-sale sign. Are you selling the house?" I asked.

"The property. I decided ten acres is too much to keep up with. I talked Dad into letting me sell five. He said he'd only agree to it if it was someone he knew who wanted to buy. Thankfully, the Morris family from down the road were looking for an extra piece of property to put a couple of horses on."

"Awesome. I'm sure that's a load off your shoulders."

"Oh, honey, you have no idea. Just the time alone I'd save not mowing it all would be worth it. I hired someone to do it when I could, but lately I haven't been able to afford it. Which means I've had to do it all by myself. It's too much. I can't do it anymore. So, I decided the best thing to do was to sell it. I plan to put the money I make from the sale into the house to spruce it up a bit. There are so many repairs that need to be done." She smoothed a hand over her face. "I don't even know where to start. If you know anyone who could use a little extra work and is good with a hammer, let me know."

I pushed the screen door open and stepped onto the porch. Only one person popped into my head. His name passed from my lips before I had time to think about whether offering his services was a good idea. "Eli Vargas is handy with carpentry stuff. He's renting out one of the old trailers in the park. He's done a lot to the place in the last couple of weeks. I know he works nights at Eddie's bar, but I'm sure he'd be interested in helping you."

"You know, I think I already knew he was good with a hammer. I'm not sure why he slipped my mind."

"If I see him on my way home I'll be sure and give him your number." Again, I wasn't sure why I was offering.

Maybe deep down my subconscious was wanting an excuse to see him again.

"Thank you, that would be great," Betty Sue said. "Need any help getting your dad to the car?"

I shook my head. This time wouldn't be as difficult as the last few. He wasn't nearly as lit.

"I'm okay." I maneuvered around Hershel's extended legs and headed for my dad's side. "Come on, let's get you home. Hershel and Betty Sue have a long road trip to pack for."

"Yeah, yeah I know. Hershel's been talking about it for days," Dad grumbled. He reached for his cane and used it to pull himself up into a standing position. I waited for him to show signs of a struggle before I reached out to help.

"Dad, dinner is done if you're ready to eat before we leave," Betty Sue said as she proceeded to help her drunken father out of his rocker as well.

"I ain't hungry," Hershel muttered while swatting her hand away.

"You sure? I made your favorite—roast beef with potatoes and carrots," she said. I grinned at her approach to coax her dad to eat as I helped mine down the porch steps. "You know I'm not stopping. It's a one-shot trip. Five hours there, which is five hours without food," Betty Sue insisted.

"Did you say roast beef with potatoes and carrots? Let me get myself a plate," Hershel pulled open the screen door and disappeared inside. "See you two later. Take care of yourself, Bill."

"Will do," Dad grunted as he made it down the final step. He tripped at the bottom when his cane became wedged between two large chunks of gravel in the driveway. I helped him right himself and then opened my passenger door by pushing the button in and pulling up before jerking it open. I really need to get the dang thing fixed.

"Bye, Betty Sue. Thanks for calling me to come get him." I waved to her while starting around the front of my car while Dad situated himself in the passenger seat. "Have a great trip."

"Thanks, sweetie. Don't forget to give that oldest Vargas boy my number. I'll pay him well to help with the repairs around this place."

"I won't. I'm sure I'll run into him sometime soon." It was more of an understatement than anything. The Universe always seemed to be pulling us together and since the full moon and him kissing me, I'd been finding it harder to stay away from him.

Once I situated myself behind the steering wheel of my car, I cranked the engine. It sputtered a few times before finally catching.

"Damn, this thing sounds horrible," Dad said. There was amusement laced in his words that irked me.

"Yeah, I know." I clamped my lips together before I said something that would start an argument between us and made a mental note to put in an early request at the next full moon for him to do repairs on it. Near a full moon was the only time he sobered up.

My cell chimed with a new text. I glanced at it in the cup holder. It was from Becca. I scooped it up and read what she'd said.

I'm getting ready to pick up Ridley and then head to the store so we can get her a sleeping

bag. I need to pick up some other supplies I'm sure the boys will end up forgetting, too. Want me to swing by and pick you up?

I quickly typed out a message letting her know I was busy right now but could meet her at the store in a few. Then asked which one she was going to. As I shifted into reverse and turned around in Betty Sue's driveway, I tried to remember if I had a sleeping bag still. I used to have one. It was turquoise with white daisies. I wasn't sure if it was still around or if Gran had donated it a while back. If she had, there was a hundred bucks tucked in my underwear drawer that I could spare some of for a decent sleeping bag.

Unless Alec wanted to share his with me...

5

It didn't take long to get from Betty Sue's house to my place, but I probably should have told Becca I'd be longer than thirty minutes. While it should have been possible since I hadn't hit every red light on the way home and I'd drove over the speed limit, I hadn't factored in how slow my dad moved while drunk.

I left the engine of my car running and hopped out to help him, but he waved my hands away.

"I don't need your damn help," he mumbled. "I can do this on my own. I have a million times."

When he missed the first step, I reached out and steadied him anyway. The front door creaked open. Gran stood in its threshold, her thin lips pinched into a frown as she watched her inebriated son wobble up the porch steps with the help of her granddaughter.

"I picked him up at Betty Sue's," I told her as I pressed my palms flat against Dad's back making sure he didn't fall backward while going up the stairs. "Sorry to dump him on you and run, but I'm supposed to meet the girls. We're going shopping for camping stuff for tonight."

While I had mentioned camping, I hadn't mentioned there would be guys coming too. She didn't need to know. I was eighteen, after all.

"All right, that's fine. You go right ahead. Enjoy yourself, honey," Gran insisted. "I'll take it from here."

"You don't need to take nothin'. I'm fine," Dad growled as he fumbled through the front door.

My gut twisted. Should I hang around for a while? It didn't seem right dropping Dad off and then leaving so soon. Not when he wasn't situated in his room first or on the couch. What if Gran had trouble getting him settled? What if he fell and she couldn't help him up?

I glanced around, searching for Gracie. While I didn't want her to be privy to our dad in all of his drunken splendor, at least with her home Gran would have help if she needed it.

"Where's Gracie?" I asked.

"She went to the movies with some friends," Gran said as Dad mumbled something about her leaving him be.

I frowned. Had Gracie really went to the movies with her friends or with Cooper Vargas? Eli's little brother was a good kid, but it didn't mean I wanted him dating my little sister. Thirteen was too young to start dating.

"He'll be fine. I'll be fine. Get out of here. Go have fun," Gran said as she shooed me off the porch.

"I'll be home in an hour or so. I still need to pack," I said as I backtracked down the steps.

"Have fun." Gran closed the door, ending the conversation.

"Love you too," I muttered unbelieving the way she'd dismissed me.

I rounded my car, heading for the driver's seat and noticed immediately the stupid thing was no longer running.

Crap.

When was the last time I'd filled the tank up? I couldn't remember. I slipped behind the steering wheel and turned the key in case running out of gas wasn't the problem and it had shut off on its own. A clicking noise sounded but the car never fully committed to starting. What was wrong with it now? I leaned back in my seat and blew out a long breath, fighting against the anger bubbling through me.

I hated my car. Hardcore freaking hated it.

I mentally counted to ten before I tried the key again. The same clicking noise came from beneath the hood.

Shit. Was my car dead? For real dead?

It had been on the fritz for a while, but I didn't think it would actually take a complete dump on me so soon. Daring to believe it wouldn't, I tried one last time to start the engine. I got the same result. My hands gripped the steering wheel so tight my knuckles turned white as I gritted my teeth together and shook back and forth while growling. I couldn't believe this was happening.

I had no car.

I reached for my cell once I calmed down a bit, deciding it was probably best if I told Becca and Ridley I was having car trouble and that I would just catch up with them later. There was no point in having them double back to pick me up. It was too late. They were probably already in the store halfway finished with their shopping. As I typed out a message to Becca a familiar voice called out to me.

"Need me to jump you off, Mina?"

I glanced up from my cell to find Eli strutting toward me. Dressed in a pair of khaki cargo shorts that looked like they'd seen better days, a gray cotton tank top, and a pair flip-flops he looked as though he'd just rolled out of bed. Even so, I'd never seen him look sexier. The sight of him had my heart pounding out of its normal rhythm and my mouth going dry.

"Maybe," I said ignoring the way his words could be seen as a sexual innuendo.

"Try it again." He stopped at the front of my car and popped the hood with ease, his fingers knowing exactly where the latch was.

I licked my lips and forced myself to focus on the situation at hand instead of him. I held my breath as I reached for my key, hoping the engine cranked over this time without issue.

It didn't.

The same clicking noise sounded, causing my heart to deflate.

"Sounds like it's the battery. I'd say you need a jump. Let me get my truck and cables." He jogged toward his trailer. I took in his broad shoulders and tight behind.

The first flickers of panic hit me as soon as he disappeared inside. What was wrong with me? Why was I suddenly so attracted to him?

I closed my eyes and leaned against my seat while I tried to get a grip on the ripples of desire for him pulsing through me. I'd be lying if I said I'd never felt a sense of attraction toward Eli Vargas, but what I'd felt lately—since he'd kissed me—was intense as well as a whole new level of scary. The pull toward him had always freaked me out, it was why I'd forced as much distance between us all these years. I was too afraid of it.

But now, it had become so much harder to ignore and push away.

In fact, I was beginning to realize I wasn't as strong as I'd once thought.

A screen door slammed shut and Eli darted toward his truck. I watched him as he climbed behind the wheel. His beast of a truck roared to life without issue and he turned it around, making his way to my piece of junk car.

"Let me hook it up and then we'll let it sit for a minute before we try again," he insisted once he'd parked in front of my car and gotten out to pop the hood of his truck.

"Thanks." There was a wild note whirling in the pitch of my voice I didn't like. It revealed too much of what I was feeling for him in the moment. At least to my ears. Eli didn't seem to notice.

I eased out of my car and erased the text I'd planned to send to Becca before beginning a new one. I told her my car battery was dead and I was getting it jumped off. That I'd be there soon. She replied back within seconds.

No problem. Take your time.

Thanks. - Mina

As I shoved my cell in my back pocket, my gaze drifted to Eli. He chewed the inside of his cheek while making sure the clamps for his cables were secured in place. I loved the way he did that. It was when I knew he was seriously concentrating on something. Once he thought they were okay, he lifted his gaze to meet mine.

"You look like you're in a hurry to get somewhere." A

shit-eating grin spread across his face. One that had me thinking he enjoyed seeing me late for something.

"I am. I'm supposed to meet up with Becca and Ridley. We're picking up camping supplies for tonight."

His face darkened. "Camping? Where are you camping at? Not out there, right?" He nodded toward the woods that kissed the trailer park.

"Yeah. Those woods."

"It's just going to be you and the girls' though right? None of the guys?" His voice had turned cold.

Was he jealous or concerned? It was hard to tell from the look on his face.

"Why does it matter to you?" I knew why it might, but asked anyway.

"It matters. Trust me," he insisted.

Charged tension formed in the space between us. Eli crossed his arms over his solid chest and narrowed his eyes on me.

"It shouldn't. I can take care of myself." My stomach churned. I knew that wasn't the truth. Not when it came to Shane and his brothers.

"There's no question, but this situation is something different altogether, Mina. You know that." He said the words slowly, emphasizing each one. "Are the guys going camping tonight with you?"

"Yes, the guys will be there." My eyes never wavered from his, but my heart rate spiked. What was he going to do? Tell me I couldn't go? He wasn't my Alpha.

He wasn't my anything.

That was a lie. Eli was a friend, if nothing else.

"We did say scoping out Shane and his brothers was a

good idea." I reminded him. "We agreed I'd hang around him and see if I can learn anything that might be helpful in finding Glenn. Camping is a good opportunity." I kept my voice down in case there was anyone within range of our conversation. Everyone in the pack still suspected Glenn had gotten sick of Taryn and left town for a while. No one thought he'd been abducted.

"No, it's not. It's suicidal, especially after what we know. You've been Moon Kissed, Mina. Don't toss yourself at their feet." Goose bumps spread across my skin at the raw emotion laced in his words.

He was worried about me. Eli Vargas was legitimately worried about me.

"I'm not," I whispered.

Tossing myself at their feet wasn't my intention at all.

"You heard Drew same as I did. You're exactly what he's looking for." Eli ran a hand through his hair as his gaze dropped to the gravel road we stood on. His jaw worked back and forth as he seemed to be contemplating his next words carefully. "I don't think it's smart. You shouldn't be spending time with Shane in the woods at night but I know I can't stop you. You're going to do whatever you want. It's how you've always been." His words were harsh, but not as harsh as his gaze when he lifted his eyes to lock with mine.

Fury roared under my skin. He made me sound selfish and rude.

"You're right. I'd still go no matter what you said." Didn't he see that I had to? Shane would think it was suspicious if I backed out now. He'd think he'd intimidate me somehow. That he'd won.

Plus, I couldn't blow Alec off again. He didn't deserve it.

Maybe I was selfish, but only when it came to him. I didn't want to give him up. He brought out a different side of me. One I happened to like.

"I knew you'd say that." Amusement that surprised me shifted through Eli's bright green eyes and the corners of his lips twisted into the ghost of a smile. "Same as you knew I'd tell you there's no way in hell you'll be out there alone with them tonight."

I blinked. "What do you mean?"

"I have to work, but I'll be sending Tate into the woods to watch over you."

I kept my face neutral. While I should have known he would do something like that, I hadn't. Eli had caught me off guard. Tension released from my muscles I hadn't been aware I'd harbored until that very second. I was glad Eli was sending someone from the pack to watch over me tonight, even if it was only Tate. At least someone would be there if things went south.

"Whatever. I'm not even going to try to fight you on this because I know there isn't a chance in hell I'd win," I said hoping I was able to keep every ounce of relief out of my voice when I spoke and still sound slightly pissed off.

I walked to the hood of my car. I didn't know what I was looking at, but knew I needed distance between us.

Eli crept up behind me. His scent saturated the air around me, causing my heart to flutter and lungs to forget how to breathe.

"Damn right," he whispered against my ear before maneuvering around me to get behind the wheel of my car. "Step back. I'm going to try it."

I took a shaky step back still able to feel his hot breath

against my ear. My entire body seemed to tremble in reaction to the sensation. A whining noise filled the air, drawing my attention to the here and now. My car was making a new noise. No more clicking. That had to be a good sign, right?

"Almost," Eli said.

He cranked the engine again. This time the noise seemed to drag on forever before it finally caught and my car revved to life again. A wide smile spread across my face.

"Yes! Thank you!" I shouted out as I rushed to the driver side door.

Eli slipped from behind the wheel. "You're welcome." He maneuvered around me to the front of my car where he unhooked the cables. "I think you're going to need a new battery, though." He called over the noise of my running engine.

Crap. There went my sleeping bag money.

"How much do they cost?" I'd never had to buy one before.

"Let me give you a ride to wherever you need to go. While I'm out I'll pick up the right battery and install it for you."

He didn't have to do that. "That would be great, but umm—"

"I'll pay for it, too." Eli slammed the hood of my car down and moved to unhook his truck. "All I ask...is that you make grilled cheese and tomato soup for us one night soon." He glanced over his shoulder at me. His lips hooked into a half smirk.

I didn't know what to say. A new battery for grilled cheese and tomato soup? It seemed like a good deal, too good of a deal. If only it wasn't coming from Eli. I didn't think spending time alone with him was a great idea, especially when there wasn't anything pack related to discuss.

Was there a way I could turn it into a pack thing?

"Obviously from the look on your face that's not in my cards," Eli said as he slammed the hood of his truck down. "I must be pushing my luck. The offer to take you wherever you're supposed to meet your friends still stands, though. I'll even get you a battery still if you give me the money."

"That's the thing, I'm not sure I have the money to cover a battery." My face shifted through at least ten shades of red. Admitting I was broke never got any easier.

"Then I guess the only way you're going to get one today is if you agree to make me a grilled cheese and tomato soup for dinner one night."

Damn him. He wasn't going to let that go, was he?

My car was my freedom. The only piece I had. Not being able to leave when I wanted would suck. Gran wouldn't give me any money for a battery. She'd make me work for it doing off the wall chores. Dad wouldn't lend me money either, and he damn sure wouldn't let me use his truck until I could save enough for a new battery.

I was screwed.

Unless...

"Fine I'll make you tomato soup and grilled cheese sometime soon. Take me to Walmart, please," I muttered as I grabbed my wallet from inside my car and cut the engine.

Eli grinned as I strode past him to climb into the cab of his truck. He slipped behind the wheel without a word and shifted into reverse.

"Does tomorrow night work for you? It works for me," he said as he made his way out of the trailer park.

"I didn't know you would give me a specific date." My words were harsh. I wasn't sure if it was because I was upset with him for gloating, or if I was upset with myself for the tiny butterflies of excitement bursting through my stomach at the thought of being alone with him.

"And time," Eli insisted. "Seven o'clock. I should be home by then. I've got a side job to do since it's my night off from Eddie's."

I ignored him, but made a mental note of the time. "Oh, speaking of side jobs, Betty Sue wants you to call her. She's selling half her property and putting the money from the sale back into her house. She needs a handyman to fix the place up and you were the first person to come to mind. I told her I'd speak with you about it."

"Glad to know I'm always so front and center in your mind," he said. "I'll give her call."

I shifted to glance out the passenger window, ignoring his jab. He turned the radio up and drove toward Walmart. When we were nearly there, I reached for my cell and sent Becca another text letting her know I was close. She messaged back saying to look for them in the camping section. My gaze drifted back out the windows as two things bounced through in my head: how nervous I was to spend the night in the woods while Shane's would be there too, and how stupid it was of me to agree to dinner with Eli tomorrow night.

I hoped I was able to dig something new up on Shane or one of his brothers so Eli and I would have something pack related to discuss. If not, I wasn't sure how the night might unfold.

6

I loaded my backpack down with a clean change of clothes, snacks, and the sleeping bag I'd bought while shopping with Becca and Ridley. Afterward, I glanced around my room looking for anything I might have forgotten. It didn't matter really, because even if I did forget something I could always run home and get it. We were camping on Alec's uncle's property which was walking distance from my place.

"I don't think you forgot anything. It looks like you packed the whole house," Gracie said from where she lay on her bed, reading another paranormal book. Her unnamed puppy lay curled into her side.

I ignored her and skimmed over the contents of my backpack once more.

"Is your phone charged?" Gracie asked.

I glanced at my cell. "Yeah, mostly."

"Then you're good. As long as you have food, water, a

charged cell phone, and a sleeping bag you should be fine. It's only one night. Stop stalling."

My lips pinched into a thin line. Was she trying to get rid of me? Was I stalling? "I guess I'm ready then. I'll get out of your hair."

As I zipped up my backpack dread slithered through me. Even though I knew Tate would be in the woods making sure nothing happened to me tonight, my stomach still knotted with fear. I wasn't afraid of Shane, but I was scared shitless his brother Drew would be waiting for the right moment to shoot me or haul me away during the night.

What if Tate fell asleep? What if Drew saw a chance to abduct me and took it? What if he succeeded?

"Have fun," Gracie muttered as she flipped the page of her book.

"Thanks. I'll see you tomorrow." I hoped my words were true.

I slung my backpack over my shoulder and started for the hall.

Dad was on the couch, snoring as he slept off the alcohol he'd consumed with Hershel earlier. Gran was in the kitchen, chopping dried herbs and stuffing them in labeled mason jars. She had a serious apothecary pantry going after years of having her own a garden. The calming scent of lavender wafted to my nose as I passed by her.

"I'm heading out." I paused at the front door to glance back at her. She hadn't looked up from what she was doing. "Anything you need me to do before I leave?"

"I can't think of anything. Have fun, and be careful."

"I will. See you tomorrow." A basket near the front door

caught my eye. It was filled with various herb concoctions and homemade food. "Who's that for?"

"The basket? It's for Taryn. I wanted to make her something to help lift her spirits. It's almost been three weeks since Glenn took off and the poor dear is still so torn up about it."

My heart skipped a beat. Had it really been almost three weeks? It didn't seem as though it had been that long. Wow.

I thought of Taryn and how heartbroken she was still. Her sister Candace had come to town for a few days, but she hadn't had any luck in forcing the Mirror Lake police department to search for Glenn any more than Taryn had. Candace hadn't been able to persuade our Alpha to do anything either. Part of me thought it was because she didn't really believe Taryn when she said Glenn was missing. Candace eventually said sided with the pack and believed Glenn had decided to up and leave. That he'd gone rogue. She'd tried to get Taryn to believe it too. Taryn didn't. In fact, I don't think she ever would. I wanted to tell her she was right not to a thousand times, but in her delicate state I thought learning the truth might be too much.

"Why don't you take the basket to her before you meet with your friends?" Gran suggested. "Saves me a walk in the hot sun."

I didn't want to, but I felt as though I should. I was headed that way anyway.

"I can do that." I picked up the basket. It was heavier than it looked. Gran had loaded it down.

"Thank you," Gran said. She went back to chopping more of her dried herbs. "Tell her I'm here if she needs anything else."

"I will."

My stomach somersaulted as I started down the stairs. I'd purposely avoided Taryn since the day I spotted her crying over Glenn. It was hard to look her in the eye knowing everything I did. Especially now that I knew she was pregnant.

I had to find out more information regarding Glenn tonight. Maybe I'd be able to get something else out of Becca. She'd dated Shane for so long she had to know something more than what she was telling me about his hunting.

"All of that for me?"

Eli stood at my car, working on something beneath the hood. I couldn't believe I'd missed him.

"What?" I asked.

He eyed the basket I held. There was a smudge of grease streaked beneath his right eye and sweat glistened across his forehead. "The basket. Is all of that for me?"

"Not unless you're pregnant," I said. "Gran made it all for Taryn."

The amusement shifting through his eyes disappeared at the mention of Taryn's name. "Oh. That was nice of her."

"Yeah, I told her I'd drop it off since it's on my way."

"Let me know how she's doing. I know my parents have been by to check on her once or twice the last couple of weeks."

"What do they have to say about her?"

Eli shrugged. "Same as everyone else I guess—how sad it is Glenn left her the way he did."

"Your parents actually by that?"

"Yeah, why wouldn't they? Glenn and Taryn didn't have the best relationship. He wasn't even a born pack member. He was a rogue before settling down with her."

I hated how Eli seemed to almost believe what he was saying. Even after everything he knew.

"Why haven't you told him anything yet? Your dad, I mean. You could have at least mentioned the possibility of something else having happened to Glenn," I whispered. "We already know what everyone believes isn't what happened. He didn't go rogue."

"Because, Mina, I already told you my dad is dealing with something big at the moment and I don't have enough proof Glenn was actually abducted for him to act on it. I can't distract him with that right now."

Anger lapped at my insides. "You have my word and your own. I know whatever evidence might've been in the woods is probably gone by now thanks to the last couple of rains we've had, but shouldn't our word count for something?"

"You know as well as I do it would count, but not for enough. He needs tangible proof before he can act. He can't just go around attacking humans who enjoy hunting in the woods behind the park."

"And what if we don't ever get any tangible proof?"

Eli's lips quirked into a slight smile. "You know as well as I do that we'll find something."

He was right. If we put our minds together we would find something.

"I'll get information tonight and then we'll get some tangible proof for your dad. Glenn has to come home. Taryn needs him. If something happened to him..." My voice shook as I spoke. I didn't like thinking about what Shane and his brothers might have done to Glenn. "Then he at least deserves to be given a proper ceremony of life from the pack."

Eli's head dipped. "I know."

The pack had traditions that needed to be upheld. We owed it to Glenn as a member of the pack to see that they happened for him if he had been killed.

"I should get this basket to Taryn and head to the camping spot I'm meeting the others at." I shifted around on my feet. "Are you sure Tate will be able to watch out for me tonight?" My voice trembled, causing me to sound like a scared little girl. I hated it.

"He'll be there. I promise you."

"Okay."

"Do you have your cell on you?"

I patted my back pocket. "Yeah."

"If anything happens, and I mean anything, don't hesitate to call me. If Tate can't get to you, I'll make damn sure someone does or else I'll come for you myself."

The tension squeezing each of my muscles dissipated. I would be protected tonight. Warmth slipped through me at the knowledge.

"Thank you," I said. Heat crept up my neck to stain my cheeks. I wasn't used to thanking anyone for help, especially not Eli.

"I mean it."

"I know." I held his gaze. "I'll talk to you later or something. I need to go."

"Yeah, okay." He nodded before turning around to focus his attention on my car again. I couldn't believe I hadn't asked what he was doing. "I'm almost done switching out the batteries. I also tightened up a couple loose bolts and changed your oil. It was like black sludge. You should have it done more often."

My mouth fell open. "You didn't have to do all that."

"I know, but I wanted to."

I smiled at him as I stepped backward in the direction of Taryn's trailer. "Thanks."

"Remember, you can thank me with tomato soup and grilled cheese tomorrow night at seven." He winked.

"Right. Tomorrow night at seven."

I turned around and hightailed it to Taryn's, knowing if I didn't I'd continue to stare at Eli all night. Even with oil and grease on him, he was still mouth-watering.

Taryn wasn't outside smoking a cigarette and crying like the last time I'd seen her. I took that as a good sign.

When I reached the door of her tiny silver bullet for a trailer, I knocked on the metal door and stepped back. No noise came from inside in response to my knock. I thought maybe she wasn't home, until I spotted her cherry red car in the driveway beside Glenn's rusty truck. His truck was a piece of junk, but Glenn worked on it almost every weekend. It still being here was the main reason Taryn believed something had happened to Glenn. She knew he'd never leave it behind if he was taking off like everyone claimed he had.

When Taryn didn't come to the door after a few more seconds, I knocked again, this time louder. Footsteps sounded from inside seconds later.

"One minute," Taryn shouted as she made her way to the door. She cracked it open and poked her head out. Her eyes were puffy and rimmed with dark circles, making her look as though she'd been crying. A lump formed in my throat. "Oh, hey," she said once she saw me.

"Hey." Words built across my tongue, but I stopped myself before they spilled out. She was probably sick of everyone asking her if she was all right. Of course she wasn't all right. Instead, I held the basket out to her. "Gran wanted me to drop this off for you. She made you a few remedies. It looks like stuff to help with morning sickness and a multivitamin tincture. She's got other goodies in here, too. Food stuff."

"Thanks." Taryn reached for the basket. "You said there's stuff for morning sickness?"

"Yeah. It's one of the brown glass bottles on top."

"Thank goodness. So far that's been the worst symptom I've had."

"I'm sure whatever Gran made will do the trick. She's pretty well known for those sorts of things." I smiled even though I didn't feel I should ever smile while in Taryn's presence. At least not until Glenn was found safe and sound and they were reunited.

"You have to tell her I said thank you," Taryn insisted.

"I will, and she wanted me to tell you if you need anything else don't hesitate to come to her." I shifted around on my feet, pulling at the straps of my backpack. I wanted to say something more, something meaningful, but nothing beautiful would come so I settled for something simple. Standard. "We're all here for you. The entire pack. Just don't... Don't forget that okay?"

A sad smile pulled at the corners of her lips as unshed tears filled her eyes. "Thank you. That means a lot to me, Mina."

I cleared my throat. Seeing her tear up was going to make me cry. "I should let you get some rest. I'm sure I'll see you around." I waved at her as I turned and headed toward the woods.

New determination to get dirt on Shane and his brothers

pulsed through me. While I enjoyed hanging out with Alec, as well as Becca and the others, tonight was also about pack related business. I needed to keep that front and center in my mind, no matter how hot Alec ended up looking chopping wood or starting a fire.

7

It didn't take long to set up our campsite. Becca, Ridley, and I each handled the finer details while the guys pitched our tents.

"Did anyone think to bring lighter fluid?" Becca asked as she placed some twigs in the fire pit. It was close to dinnertime, which meant she was probably preparing to cook us something.

"I brought a lighter, but I didn't think to bring any lighter fluid," Ridley said as she rummaged through her backpack.

"We don't need lighter fluid," Benji insisted. He stepped to the fire pit and bent at the knee. "Just give me a few dry leaves and a couple of sticks. I'll get us a fire going in no time."

"Hey, babe?" Becca called out to Shane. I'd never heard her use a term of endearment when talking to him before. It surprised me and rubbed me the wrong way. Shane wasn't who Becca thought he was. He wasn't a good guy. "Did you get the cooler from the back of your truck yet?"

"No, but I can grab it really quick. I need to get the drinks anyway," Shane said as he headed toward his truck.

Maybe I was about to see the side of Shane everyone else always did. He was being so...*normal.*

I folded out another bag chair we'd bought at the store and placed it in line with the others, making a semicircle near the fire pit. My gaze drifted to Shane. He was still at his truck getting the cooler out of the back. No matter how normal he was acting, I planned to watch him like a hawk tonight. Just in case it was all an act and he was trying to get me to let my guard down while in his presence.

Shane heaved not one, but two coolers from the back of his truck and carried them to where Becca was. If he noticed me staring at him he didn't let on. Instead, he hummed the melody to a song I didn't recognize while he walked. The more I watched him the more uneasy I felt. It was odd and off-putting to see him in such a good mood. I was used to him being a jerk when I was around. I understood more than anyone how spending time in nature could ease away a person's troubles, but this was nuts. He was too happy. What could he possibly be so happy about? My skin crawled as possible reasons for his happiness filled my mind.

My gaze drifted to the edge of the woods. I skimmed them, searching for signs of Tate. Was he out there yet? Eli had promised he'd be there making sure I was okay tonight. When though? Once night had fallen so he'd be hidden better?

Even though I would never admit it out loud, I wished Tate was here now. I couldn't feel him, though.

"Here's the cooler with food and here's the one with

drinks," Shane said as he lifted the lid on the second cooler to reveal the inside. Ice covered a variety of beverages, but none of them were soda. "Pick your poison ladies and gents," he said as a wicked grin spread across his face.

"What did you bring?" Benji craned his neck to see inside the cooler from where he was attempting to start a fire.

"Beer. There's a variety. I had Drew buy them for me last night." Shane grabbed a long neck bottle from the cooler and shifted to face me. Chunks of ice and droplets of water fell from the dark glass as he held it out to me. The wicked grin on his face widened, making him look creepy. "Here, I figured you'd like this one. You know, since you seem to have such an obsession with the moon."

Pinpricks of unease traveled along my spine. It hadn't taken him long to take a jab at me.

I frowned as I took the bottle from him. My eyes dipped to the label. *Blue Moon*.

"Funny," I muttered as I glanced around at the others. My heart rate spiked. Had they noticed he was calling me out in front of them?

"Come on. Drink up." Shane nodded to the beer in my hand. "Tonight is going to be fun."

Fun? I hadn't known the word was a part of his vocabulary until now.

I twisted the cap off, but didn't take a sip. Drinking around him didn't seem like the best idea, but I didn't think he would stop staring at me until I at least opened the thing.

"What's this?" Alec asked as he dropped the twigs and sticks he gathered from the woods on top of the pile he'd gathered earlier. His attention was fixated on Shane. "I leave for all of two minutes for more firewood and come back to see you trying to get my girl drunk?"

"Nope, not just your girl. Everyone. I made sure I got enough for all of us to last through the night." Shane grinned.

Alec glanced inside the cooler. "Damn, you aren't kidding."

"I'll take one." Becca surprised me by saying. I hadn't pegged her as the type to drink.

"What kind do you want?" Shane asked her.

"Whatever you gave Mina is fine."

Shane reached into the cooler and found another Blue Moon. He twisted the cap off before passing it to Becca. She lifted up onto the tips of her toes and kissed him.

"Thanks," I heard her whisper before sitting in one of the bag chairs I'd set out. She motioned for me to sit in the one beside her. Once I'd stepped to where she was, she held her beer out to me. "To camping."

I clinked my beer to hers. "To camping."

We both took a sip. The entire time I could feel Shane's eyes on me from where he stood a few feet away. I risked a glance at him. There was something sinister flashing through his eyes. If I hadn't witnessed him opening my beer and known he hadn't done anything to it before passing it my way, I would have thought he had. Maybe he thought he was about to get me drunk.

Not going to happen.

"Bottom's up," Shane said. There was something predatory in his eyes.

A shiver slipped along my spine. Agreeing to this night was a bad idea. I could feel it in my gut. Shane was too attentive to me. He was too chipper as well. Something was definitely up and my wolf was practically begging me to get the hell out of here.

Alec stepped to my side. He placed a kiss on my temple as he slipped an arm around my waist. The sharp scent of beer from his breath wafted to my nose. I'd never seen him drink alcohol before. Just like Becca, he didn't seem as though he was the type.

"Having fun?" he asked.

"Yeah, and the night is just getting started," I said without taking my eyes off Shane. His eyes grew dark as his jaw clenched. Did he not like me being so close to Alec?

If I hadn't known any better, I would have thought Shane had a thing for Alec. That was far from the truth, though. Shane just didn't want his best friend dating a werewolf.

"Benji, need some help with that fire, man?" Alec asked as he released me and started to where he was struggling to get a fire started.

"Everything is too damn wet out here," Benji grumbled.

I sat in the chair near Becca.

"I didn't know you drank," I said, trying to forget about the way Shane kept staring at me.

"Normally I don't, but I figured what the heck. Summer is halfway over. Soon I'll be stressed out from school again. Might as well enjoy myself some before college starts." She shrugged.

"I know what you mean," I said as I took another sip. Surprisingly it tasted good, but I wasn't about to get tipsy tonight. Not with Shane around. Maybe I could make this beer last me all night without anyone noticing.

Ridley moved to sit in the chair beside me. Her gaze was focused on the woods in front of us. I tried to follow her stare, but didn't see whatever it was she seemed to. It didn't mean there wasn't anything there, though. It was possible her witchy side was seeing something I couldn't. Or maybe she'd spotted Tate? I skimmed over the greenery and brush again but didn't see anything. I opened my mouth to ask her if she was okay, but Benji had stepped behind her. He passed a beer in front of her face. She flinched, causing Benji to laugh.

"Sorry," he chuckled. "I didn't mean to scare you."

"It's okay." Her face shifted through at least five shades of red as she took the beer from him. She never put it to her lips. Unease rippled from her as her gaze darted back to the woods. I wanted to ask what she was looking at, but figured it had to be Tate. I didn't want to blow his cover. "Thanks"

"And...let there be fire," Alec said as crackling embers floated toward the sky from the fire pit in front of me. None of these guys were boy scouts, that was for sure. It had taken them way too long to start a fire.

"Awesome," Benji said as he gave him a high five. "You know, we should have brought our fishing poles. No better time to fish than at night."

The guys drifted into a conversation about fishing, and Becca began rifling through the cooler of food. I took the opportunity to chat with Ridley.

"You know, you don't have to drink that." I nodded to the untouched beer in her hand.

"I know." She trailed her thumb along the side of the bottle, wiping away the condensation building. "I will, it's just..."

"What? Is something wrong?" If having Tate in the woods freaked her out so much maybe I should tell her why he was there. Or at least something about him being safe even if I couldn't tell her the exact reason why he was hiding in the woods, watching.

Ridley's blue eyes shifted to mine. Her pupils were dilated as she bit her bottom lip. "It's this place. Something about it gives me the heebie-jeebies."

A witch telling me something about this place was giving her the heebie-jeebies creeped me out.

"Why?" I asked as I took another sip from my beer. My mouth had gone dry.

Ridley adjusted her glasses higher on her nose as she contemplated her next words. "I can't say for sure, but there's something about it I can't shake."

"Like a feeling?" I needed more details. Was it something she felt or something she saw?

"It's going to sound crazy, but I get the impression you're capable of handling crazy for some reason," she said, holding my gaze. I wanted to tell her she had no idea how much crazy I could handle but didn't. Instead, I kept my mouth shut and waited for her to continue. "I feel like...like there's tragedy lingering in the air here. I think something horrible happened in these woods not too long ago."

I couldn't breathe. Was she talking about Glenn being abducted?

"I'm probably wrong, though," she insisted with a shrug. She released a long, shaky breath before taking a sip from her beer. "Forget I said anything, okay?"

"Do you get feelings like that often?" I couldn't let what she'd said go. One, I didn't want her thinking I thought she was crazy. Two, I wanted to know how what she felt worked. I wanted her to elaborate.

"Ever since I was little."

"Hey, how many hot dogs do you think I should make?" Becca asked us. "I brought two packages, but do you really think I need to make them both?"

I hated that she'd interrupted me and Ridley's conversation, but Ridley seemed glad.

"How many come in a package?" I asked.

"Eight," Becca said as she read the front of the package. "There are six of us, but I know Shane can eat at least two and Benji might even eat three by himself."

"Then make both. That way the guys can eat as many as they want and there's still something for us," I suggested.

"I'm with Mina. Make both," Ridley insisted. She took another sip from her beer and I noticed whatever tension she'd been harboring before was slowly melting away. I liked to think it had more to do with telling me what she felt rather than her beer.

I wanted to ask her more, but didn't want her to feel as though I was putting her on the spot. It would probably be best to wait and see if she brought it up again later tonight on her own. I did, however, make a mental note to mention something about what she'd said to Eli. It was too creepy not to.

"Anyone else need a refill?" Shane asked as he made his way to the cooler. He lifted the lid and pulled another beer out for himself. "Anyone?" he asked again as he glanced at each of us.

"I'll take another," Benji said. He moved to where Shane was, squeezing Ridley's shoulder as he passed by her chair.

"Alec?" Shane asked.

"Nah, man. I'm good. Pacing myself," Alec said as he

stepped behind my chair. He leaned down and placed a kiss to the top of my head. "Still having a good time?"

"Yeah. I love this place," I said as I glanced up at him.

"I brought a pack of cards if anyone wants to play," Benji said as he rifled through the backpack he'd brought.

"I'll play," Alec grinned. "What game are we playing?"

"You name it, we'll play it." Benji removed the cards from their box and began shuffling.

Two hours later, we'd all taken part in a game of poker and the guys had played two or three games of blackjack. We'd eaten Becca's meal and each of us had gone beyond one beer. I was just starting beer number three, but Benji and Alec were already hammered. Becca wasn't far behind. It was all because of Shane. He kept passing out beers and challenging Benji and Alec to race while drinking, seeing who could down a beer the fastest. Benji won every time, but it didn't keep Alec from trying. And, it didn't take me long to realize Shane was trying to get everyone drunk.

This put me on edge.

My gaze was constantly drifting to the woods in search of some sign Tate was there. I couldn't see him or feel his presence. More times than I could count I thought to reach for my cell and message Eli to ask if Tate had made it out here yet, but always decided against it. I didn't want Eli believing I felt a need to have someone watch over me. I didn't want him to think I was scared because then he'd never let me live coming out here tonight down.

Darkness settled in and I felt my unease grow. I took another sip from my beer, knowing it would be my last of the night. I needed to keep my wits about me because Shane's looks my way had only grown more sinister as the night went on.

"I'll be right back," I said to Alec as I stood and handed him my beer. He was playing another game of blackjack with Benji. Shane was sitting this one out. I could feel his eyes on me, but I ignored them. "I need to use the restroom."

"I hate to say it, but pick a tree, darlin'," Alec said with a wide grin. His face was flushed from alcohol and his eyes were bloodshot.

"Yeah, yeah. I know." I rolled my eyes. "You guys have things so easy."

Alec didn't say anything, but instead burst into a fit of laughter as I walked away. I started into the woods, glancing around for any signs of Tate. The last thing I wanted was for him to watch me pop a squat.

I made it a few feet away from camp and hid behind a large tree. My gaze swept the woods, searching for Tate while I unbuttoned my shorts. When I didn't see him, I slipped them down along with my panties and held my breath as I released my bladder. My ears struggled to listen beyond the night noises for someone creeping up on me. As soon as I'd drip-dried, I pulled my panties and shorts up quickly, eager to get back to where everyone was at. Being separated from the others had my anxiety on high alert.

Something crashed through the woods nearby and I jumped.

"Jesus, if that was you Tate I'm going to beat the crap out of you," I growled as I swept my gaze over the area where the noise had come from.

Slight movement through the trees captured my attention,

but I couldn't make out what it was until it stepped closer. The sliver of light from the crescent moon filtering through the tree branches above glistened across dark fur. Was Tate watching me in wolf form? For whatever reason, I'd assumed he'd be in human form. I guessed wolf form made more sense, though. Then he'd be able to hear and see better. He'd also be able to do more to protect me, should the need arise.

I took a step forward, hoping to get a better glimpse of him. Tate wouldn't be able to understand me if I spoke to him —I'd learned this much the night I became Moon Kissed—but it wouldn't keep me from speaking my mind to him about sneaking up on me while I was peeing.

When he shifted further into the thicket of brush and tried to hide from my view chills ran along my spine. Was someone else watching me he didn't want to see him? I paused and glanced around. When I didn't see anyone, I continued toward him.

"What is wrong with you?" I whispered as I peeled back a few of the thinner low-hanging branches so I could get a better view of him.

I realized then I wasn't looking at Tate at all—instead, I was looking at Violet.

What was she doing out here? She knew the rules and the risks when it came to running alone. Apparently, she didn't care. Had she come out here every night since the full moon? I hoped not. Violet didn't know the dangers lurking in the woods on any given night like I did. She'd heard Gran's stories same as everyone else, but she didn't know how serious the consequences of being in these woods alone while shifted were. My stomach twisted. Violet was exactly what Drew was hoping to grab for a big chunk of money—a female werewolf.

She needed to go home. She needed to get out of here. Now.

"You shouldn't be here, Violet!" I raised my voice and waved my arms, but she didn't move. "I mean it. You need to get out of here. Now!" At the sharp sound of my voice, she turned tail and took off through the woods. I knew she wouldn't understand what I'd said to her, but she could pick up on my feelings and the tone I'd spoken in. That should be enough to have her hightailing it back to the park.

The knots in my stomach untied themselves and I exhaled a long breath at the sight of her retreating form. The sense of relief I felt didn't last long, though. Violet wasn't headed toward the trailer park like I wanted her to be, she was heading deeper into the woods.

My heart kick-started in my chest.

I pulled my cell from my back pocket and scrolled through old text messages until I found Eli's name. I didn't know who else to tell. I didn't have Tate's number and even though Eli was at work, I still felt he might be able to help. Maybe he could send a message to Tate.

I know you're working, but I just spotted Violet in the woods. She must have decided to take a run by herself. - Mina

I waited a few seconds for him to respond before I started slowly heading back to the others.

What the hell is she doing out there? She knows better than to run alone. Especially being newly changed.

Yeah, well she is. I stepped away from camp for a second to use the restroom and spotted her. At first I thought it was Tate, but then I realized it was Violet. - Mina

Movement a few feet away from me garnered my attention. The fine hair on the back of my neck stood on end. There were too many eyes out here, watching me. I could feel them all now, but I couldn't determine if they were animal or human and I knew it wouldn't be Violet again. Not after the way I'd yelled at her.

Another text came through from Eli, startling me.

I'll let Tate know she's there and see if he can get her to head home. It's not safe for her out there. We both now she's exactly what Shane and his brothers are looking for.

My heart pounded against my rib cage. I hoped Tate could find her. I needed to know she was safe at home. She was too young for whatever Shane's brother Drew had planned for a female wolf. Her parents and little sister flashed through my mind. They'd be devastated if she disappeared. Gracie would be too. Violet's younger sister, Callie, was her best friend.

Thanks. - Mina

There was nothing else left to say. Eli would message Tate and he would get Violet to go home. I had to trust in that.

My gaze swept over the woods surrounding me as I continued making my way back to our camp. I'd been gone for too long. While I was sure Alec and a few of the others might not have noticed, Shane probably would. It wasn't good for me to be out here another second alone.

A thought came to me: What if Tate was in his wolf form? There would be no way for Eli to let him know Violet was out here.

Shit.

All I could do was hope things worked out for the best, because the alternative was something I didn't want to think about.

8

When I made it back to the others they were sitting around the fire, listening to Benji tell a joke. I sat in the seat next Alec again. He glanced at me. His eyes were nearly shut, but he still managed a smile before taking another swig from his beer.

"You were gone for a while," he slurred as he reached out to drape an arm over my shoulder. I wanted to laugh, but held it in.

God, he was wasted.

"Was I?"

"Yeah. Thought I was gonna have to come look for you." He released my shoulder in favor of placing his hand on my thigh. "I'm glad you came tonight. We don't get to spend enough time together. Not as much as I'd like. I really like you. I mean, I *really freaking* like you."

His words were sweet, but I chuckled at him nonetheless. "I really freaking like you, too."

"Do you? Sometimes I wonder," he said as his bloodshot

eyes narrowed on me. "You seem distant, almost as though you're lost in your own world. One I can't join."

I licked my lips, not knowing what to say. He'd hit the nail on the head. I was lost in my own world. All the time. Unfortunately, it was one he couldn't join.

Had I really been that transparent around him, though?

"I don't mind. Not really. All I want is to get close to you, Mina. As close as you'll allow." He leaned forward until only inches remained between us. His mouth barely brushed mine when he spoke again. "You're like a freaking mystical creature, Mina Ryan, and I want to know everything about you."

My heart stopped. Was he being literal? Did he know what I was? Alarm nipped at my insides. Suddenly, I felt as though I was treading in dangerous territory with him.

Alec leaned away, giving me space to breathe but my lungs seemed to forget how. His gaze intensified and I knew the conversation wasn't over yet.

"I've been fascinated by magick and mystical creatures, the supernatural world, since I was little," he whispered before taking another swig from his beer. My throat grew dry. This conversation couldn't be going anywhere good. "I don't talk much about it because my mom hates anything supernatural related—she thinks it's all Devil's play—but after what happened to my uncle I've never been about to shake the feeling everything muttered about in this town is all real."

Oh no. Shane didn't need to hear any of this and Alec didn't need to continue with his train of thought. He might ask me a question I wouldn't be able to answer. Not here. Not now. Maybe not ever.

My gaze drifted to Shane. He wasn't paying attention to our conversation. Becca was doing a good job of occupying him with her lips. It was the first time I'd seen them look like an actual couple. Generally, Shane was too busy being moody.

When their kiss broke, Shane placed her knuckles to his lips in a sweet gesture that spurred a giggle from her and had me thinking he might be sweeter than I gave him credit for. Maybe this side of him was the one Becca and the others saw most often. Maybe I made his bad side come out. Or maybe we had more in common than I liked to think—we both had a strong desire to protect those we cared for.

My gaze drifted to Ridley and Benji. They were playing a game of war with the cards Benji had brought, oblivious to us.

"Have you ever wondered if it was all real?" Alec muttered, drawing my attention back to him. "There's no way someone could make all that crap up, right? Vampires, witches, werewolves...*fairies*. I mean, someone had to see at least one of them along the line. Humans can't have that good of imaginations. Not a chance."

I squirmed in my seat. What could I say? What *should* I say? Alec leaned back in his chair and glanced up at the night sky.

"I don't know." I shrugged. "I guess I've never given much thought to it."

Alec's head lulled to the side. His eyes were still bloodshot and glossed over but his gaze was focused directly on me. "Oh, come on. You can't be serious. You've honestly never—"

"Hey! Know what we all should do?" Benji shouted as he slapped a stack of cards down on the cooler between him and Ridley. "Go for a little nighttime swim in the lake!"

"*Yes*," Shane insisted, surprising me with his level of enthusiasm for the idea. "A moonlight swim sounds perfect."

He tapped on Becca's thigh, motioning for her to stand so he could get up. She giggled when he intertwined his fingers through hers and pulled her along with him toward the lake. Apparently, alcohol made Becca a giggly school girl without a thought of her own. I didn't think skinny dipping was something she'd be up for if she was sober.

I debated for a second on whether I should try to be her voice of reason or let her cut loose a little?

When she stumbled, tripping on a root I knew she had to be hammered. Shane caught her before she hit the ground. His reflexes were quick for being so intoxicated. The two of them burst into a fit of laughter and I rolled my eyes even as a smile stretched onto my face. Becca was having fun. She'd be okay.

Ridley caught my eye. Anxiety radiated off her. She wasn't as drunk as the others. We were both cautious tonight, albeit for different reasons.

Alec wobbled to his feet and offered me his hand. I took it. The heat from his touch seeped through my body, making me ten times hotter than I already was. Maybe a dip in the lake would do all of us some good. Heck, it might even sober everyone up.

As the six of us made our way through the woods toward the lake, we made more noise than we probably should. For me, it was on purpose. I wanted Tate to hear us and slink deeper into the shadows. If Violet was still around, I wanted her to have another reason to head home.

Once the lake came in to view, Alec let go of my hand and jogged toward the water. He stripped as he went, leaving only his boxers on. Heat simmered up my neck and across my face as I took in the sight of him. The lean muscles of his back flexed in the dim light of the moon as he moved and I found it impossible to look away from him.

"Okay, so I guess we're going swimming," Ridley muttered from beside me as she kicked off her shoes. Benji had already raced to the water and was splashing with the others.

I peeled off my shirt and tossed it onto the nearest pile of clothes. "Yeah, I guess so."

"This may sound weird," Ridley said as she slinked out of her shorts. "But I feel like if I don't say something I'm not going to be able to enjoy the rest of my night."

I shifted to glance at her. "Umm...Okay,"

She licked her lips and paused in undressing to lock eyes with me. Her dark ringlets floated around her face as a gentle breeze swept through the air. It gave her an eerie, witchy vibe that sent goose bumps prickling across my skin.

"Again, this is going to sound crazy but I've had a feeling all night that you need to be careful," she whispered. "It's a gut feeling something bad might happen to you tonight if you're not. Now that we're out here in the open it's gotten worse. Just, be careful."

"Okay." Did she get the feeling I didn't know how to swim? I did. Or was it something else?

"I know I sound nuts. You can write me off as being a mental case if you want after tonight, but I would never be able to forgive myself if I didn't tell you what I was feeling and something bad happened."

"It's okay," I said as I peeled off my shorts. "I don't think you're nuts and thanks for the heads-up." I flashed her a smile, but it was forced. All her woo-woo feeling stuff was starting to freak me out.

Tension melted from her face as she studied me. Was I the first person to take one of her warnings to heart? Maybe in the past people had treated her like a freak because of them. I didn't think she was a freak, I only felt grateful she'd said something. It confirmed I shouldn't let my guard down tonight no matter what.

I walked with Ridley to the water's edge. The others were splashing around and laughing. Alec took notice of me approaching.

"Come on in, the water's fine," he insisted as he treaded water. His eyes appraised me the way I had him seconds before. Heat bloomed across my face. Wearing nothing but my bra and underwear seemed more intimate and taboo than a bathing suit even though it covered the same areas.

I dipped my toes in the water, testing its temperature while trying to ignore the way Alec's eyes trailed over me in an unabashed way. It was cool, but not cold enough to detour me from stepping in further. Ridley walked out until her ankles were covered. A visible shiver slipped through her and I laughed.

"It's colder than I thought it would be," she said wrapping her arms over her chest.

"Yeah, but it's not that bad," I insisted.

Splashing captured my attention. Benji had dunked Alec under and Alec was struggling to retaliate. I took a few steps forward until I was knee-deep in the water and glanced back at Ridley. She looked small and frail as she chewed her bottom lip, staring at the rippling water's surface.

Did she know how to swim?

"Hey," I called out to her. "You coming?"

Her gaze lifted to mine. "Yeah. Water just isn't my thing."

"You don't have to get in if you don't want to," I insisted, debating whether I should hang back with her so she'd feel less uncomfortable.

"Oh, yes she does!" Benji shouted from somewhere behind me. He darted passed me, splashing me in the face as he went. "Just a little bit. Come on. We don't have to go out far if you don't feel comfortable, though."

My heart melted a little. I'd never thought of Benji as the sweet type. When he talked to Ridley he was never anything except sweet, though.

"I won't let anything happen to you. Promise," he said as he held out a hand to her.

"I know," I heard Ridley say before I shifted back around to let them have their moment. I made my way further out into the lake.

The water reached my waist when Alec started toward me. I paused, allowing my stomach a few seconds to adjust to the cooler temperature.

"Keep it coming," Alec coaxed. A wide smile stretched across his face and he crooked his finger at me.

I laughed and continued forward. Once we were close enough to touch, his fingertips skimmed over my waist as he gripped my hips and pulled me closer. The heat of his body pressed against me and he dipped his head to brush his lips against mine. My heart beat triple time as I moved my lips against his, relishing in the slow pace he'd set. It was tender and sweet, while at the same time fiery. My arms locked around his neck as his fingers dug into the flesh of my hips. His tongue skimmed my bottom lip, teasing me as his excitement pressed against my lower stomach. Lust clouded my thoughts. It didn't last long. Soon a prickling sensation spread across my skin as the feeling I was being watched rushed through me.

I reined myself in, or at least I tried to. Alec wouldn't allow it, though. His grip on me tightened as he pushed our kiss toward something deeper and more passionate. The tender slip of his tongue across mine became primal and sexy, causing every thought to evaporate from my mind. It was all-consuming the way he kissed me. I could think of nothing else besides him.

The way he tasted. The way he smelled. The way he touched me.

In that moment, there was only Alec and me. No one else.

Hopefully whoever was watching us would look away.

9

I grabbed the grocery bag I'd tossed in the fridge earlier. "I won't be home for dinner tonight," I said to Gran as I closed the fridge. "I'm eating with a friend."

"A friend? What friend?" Suspicion laced Gran's words.

"Yeah. Who is this friend, Mina?" Gracie asked. She sounded as though she knew more than she was letting on.

I pursed my lips together. They both knew who but neither were going to let me go without saying his name.

"Eli," I muttered.

Gracie wiggled her eyebrows at the mention of his name. "That's who I thought you were eating with tonight." She shifted her attention to Gran. "She's cooking dinner for him. That's what the stuff she bought is for."

"How do you know?" I hadn't mentioned anything to her. Heck, I hadn't said a word to anyone about our plans tonight.

"I know things." Gracie folded her arms across her chest as a smug look stretched across her face.

"Yeah, right." Eli must've told his brothers we were

hanging out tonight.

I wasn't sure how this made me feel.

"Cooper told me," Gracie confessed. "Eli and Cooper were supposed to do something tonight, but Eli canceled because he said you were coming over to cook for him." A stupid grin curved at the corners of her lips. She obviously thought there was more to the night than dinner.

There wasn't.

"You're spending the night with Eli then?" Gran asked. Amusement twisted through her words.

"What? No! I never said anything about spending the night with him. I'm making him dinner. Nothing more." I corrected her. My hands grew clammy and my face too warm.

"Sounds like a date," Gran insisted with a grin.

"It's not."

"If you want to spend the night with him, you'd be allowed," Gran said as though she hadn't heard me.

My fingernails bit into the palms of my hands. "I don't want to spend the night with him, Gran."

"All I'm saying is if you want to, you can."

"Oh, I'm sure she wants to," Gracie snickered.

"You two are impossible." I swiped the bread I'd bought earlier off the counter and started toward the front door. "I'm not spending the night with him. I'm cooking him dinner as payment for what he did for me the other day."

"And what might that be," Gran asked.

I paused and glanced back at her. She stood in the kitchen, prepping whatever meal she'd intended to cook tonight for us all. "My car wouldn't start so he jumped it off. It was clear it wouldn't last, so he offered to give me a ride to where I was going. He bought me a battery, fixed a couple of things on my car, and changed my oil. The deal was, I would owe him dinner. Nothing more. Nothing less." I twisted the knob on the front door and stepped outside into the humid air. Gran said something, but I was done with the conversation. It had me feeling uncomfortable in my own skin. Mainly because I'd had such a great time with Alec last night guilt was threatening to overtake me. I attempted to shake it off as I cut through the thick air and headed straight for Eli's trailer, carrying the groceries for his grilled cheese and tomato soup.

For once, the Bell sisters weren't on their porch. Today's high temperature must have been too much. It was sweltering out. My cell said it was ninety-seven earlier. While I thought the heat had begun to taper off, it was still so humid out it was almost hard to breathe. My tank top stuck to me and the backs of my knees began to sweat as I walked. I picked up my pace, eager to be out of the sizzling sun.

A low humming grabbed my attention as I reached Eli's trailer. An AC unit stuck out the living room window. It looked brand-new. There were no dents in it and it wasn't covered in pollen and dirt from years of use like the hunk of junk that hung in our living room window. A wide grin sprang onto my face at the promise of actual chilled air. I almost forgot to knock. I caught myself before I twisted the knob to let myself in and rapped my knuckles against the door instead.

Footsteps sounded from inside. The instant the door opened cold air washed over me, making it easy to breathe again. I closed my eyes, basking in the sensation of goose bumps erupting across my skin from the contrast of temperatures I was feeling. Cold on my front, heat on my behind.

"Hey. Come on in," Eli said as a breath of amusement escaped him. I opened my eyes, knowing I looked crazy but not caring. The cool air felt too good. "I see you're already enjoying my new luxury."

I hurried inside and Eli closed the door behind me, sealing in the icy air. "Oh yeah. I can't believe how humid it is out there today."

"I know. Figured this would come in handy more than a couch."

I stepped into the kitchen and placed my bags on the countertop. "Priorities."

"Exactly. Sometimes you have to choose which level of comfort you're ready to sacrifice in order to gain another. In this case, I'm fine sitting on the floor if it means I get to beat the heat wave."

"Did you get one for every room or just in here?" I asked as I pulled my groceries from the bag and set them out on the counter.

"Every room. Well, not the bathroom, but I didn't think it mattered." He crossed into the kitchen.

"That's awesome. I wish Gran would get one for me and Gracie's room. It's hot and stuffy in there at night."

"Yeah, I can't stand being hot when I'm trying to sleep."

"Me either. That's why I put a box fan in the window and crank it to high. Sometimes it helps, sometimes it doesn't." I crumbled the plastic grocery bag up and tossed it in the trash. "So, do you have a pot for the soup and a pan for me to cook the grilled cheeses in?"

Eli maneuvered around me to retrieve what I'd asked for from a cabinet. His masculine scent wafted to my nose, causing my nerve endings to catch fire with want. I took a step back, putting distance between us. He didn't seem to notice. When he came up holding a pot and pan, I quickly took them and shifted to face the stove.

"How did everything go last night?" Eli asked.

It was a question I'd been expecting, but not one I cared to answer. Talking about Alec with Eli seemed wrong. On more than one level.

I bypassed thoughts of Alec and the kiss we'd shared in the lake while trying to focus on things that pertained to Glenn's disappearance or anything that could be pack related.

"Eh," I shrugged.

"What's that mean?"

Had Tate not filled him in on things? "I wasn't able to get any new information on Shane and his brothers."

"Nothing?"

I shook my head. "No. And before you say anything let me let me tell you why. I hoped I'd be able to get Becca talking again, but Ridley was there. Becca and me didn't have a chance to chit-chat like normal."

At the mention of Ridley, I remembered the weird things she'd said to me.

"By the way, do you know anything about the Caraways?" I asked.

"What do you mean? I know they're witches. The oldest witch family in Mirror Lake, actually," he said as he watched me get out a stick of butter and begin rubbing it along the hot pan.

"I know that much. Ridley is new, though. She moved here at the beginning of the school year. I'm not sure she has the same magick as the others. Do you know anything about her? I know your dad keeps in close contact with the Caraways."

"He keeps close contact with all supernaturals in town," Eli corrected.

"Right." Why did I get the feeling Eli was hinting at there being more supernaturals here than what I'd grown up knowing about? Where there more than the witches and vampires living in Mirror Lake?

There couldn't be any more vampires than the one family. The Caraway witches would only allow the Montevallo family to reside in Mirror Lake. Any others were driven out by us. It was part of the deal we had going with the Caraway witches. They cloaked our ritual grounds so humans and others wouldn't be able to harm us or witness our ceremonies. In return, we were to keep vampires who weren't a part of the Montevallo vampire family away. I wasn't one hundred percent sure why the witches wanted vampires banned from Mirror Lake, but I'd heard once it was because they held the power to compel witches to do their bidding, and the Caraway witches didn't want to be controlled. I understood. I wouldn't want a bloodsucker to control me either.

As for the Montevallo family, they didn't live here at the moment. In order to keep suspicion from humans away they moved around often. I hadn't seen them myself, but Gran had. Once.

"Does your dad know anything about Ridley?" I bypassed the questions forming in my head about what other supernaturals might be living in my town and went directly to what I wanted to know more about—what powers did Ridley Caraway have?

"She has magick, if that's what you're asking," Eli said. "It's not as powerful as the others, though. Not yet, anyway. She's a Caraway witch, but her bloodline was passed to her through her father. If it had come from a female born Caraway she'd be much stronger. Her father was Rowena's sister. Why?"

"She said some strange things to me last night." I laid two slices of bread in the pan with the melted butter, allowing them to soak in some of the butter and toast before placing two slices of cheese on one. A good grilled cheese was made with two slices and loads of butter. That was the secret.

"What did she say to you?" Concern flared through his words. It had me looking away from the sandwich I was cooking to meet his stare.

"Nothing bad. Just something about how she could feel tragedy in the air when we were in the woods."

"Okay." Eli leaned against the counter beside me and folded his arms across his solid chest. Electricity pulsed to life across my skin nearest him. "I mean, that is where Glenn was abducted. We know from the blood and signs of struggle he wasn't taken willingly, he'd been injured. Tragedy in the air might describe that section of woods well."

"I guess." I tried to ignore what he was making me feel and added more butter to the pan I was cooking his sandwich in. "The way she looked when she said it left an uneasy feeling in the pit of my stomach, though."

"Understandable." He started to say something else, but paused when he saw me gearing up to say something else. "What? She said something else?"

"She warned me I should be careful."

"Of what?"

I shrugged and then tried to cram two more slices of bread into the tiny pan. "She said she couldn't pinpoint exactly what I needed to be careful of, but she'd feel bad if something happened to me and she didn't warn me. There was something about last night that gave her a bad feeling." I thought about adding how she'd said it after we had all been drinking and went for a swim in the lake, but decided to keep that to myself. Knowing I'd been drinking while in the presence of Shane wasn't going to sit well with Eli.

A sigh escaped him. His warm breath floated over the side of my face as he leaned closer to me. "I wasn't going to say anything about this because I didn't want you to be afraid, but somebody was in the woods last night and it wasn't just Tate and Violet."

A shiver slipped along my spine. "What do you mean?"

"I mean, somebody tranquilized Tate. Shot him in the ass, actually." A smirk twisted Eli's lips as he ran a hand through his dark hair.

"Is he okay?" Thickness built in the back of my throat.

I knew someone had been watching me. When we were swimming in the lake I'd felt someone's eyes. Stupidly, I'd thought it was Tate. Now that I knew it hadn't been him but someone else, my skin crawled.

Eli nodded. "Yeah, he's okay. A little groggy and dizzy this morning, but after a couple hours it should wear off."

"Do you think it was Shane's brothers?" I asked as I flipped our grilled cheeses over again.

"I do. I don't think they were after Tate either," Eli insisted. His voice had turned cold, causing fear to clench my gut. I had a feeling I knew what he'd say next. "I think they were after you, Mina."

All the breath left my lungs. I shifted to face the stove entirely, not wanting him to see the panic I was feeling reflected on my face. My eyes unfocused as I thought back to the sensation of someone watching me multiple times during the night and Ridley's warning. "Do you think that's what Ridley was trying to tell me? That Shane's brothers were in the woods, waiting for an opportunity to abduct me?"

"It seems likely." Fury rippled from him. It pressed against me, heating my skin.

I left the stove and placed as much distance between me and Eli as his small kitchen would allow while I searched for a can opener. A rusted one in the last drawer was all I found. Eli grabbed the can of soup before I could, and pulled the tab up on the top I hadn't noticed. It popped open and he handed it to me. The scent of tomatoes and basil wafted to my nose. It was a familiar scent. One that should bring me comfort, but didn't.

Suddenly, I wasn't hungry.

I dumped the soup into the heated pot. The more I thought about Tate being tranquilized, the more I wondered why I was still here. Why hadn't they taken me once he was out of the way?

"After they took out Tate why didn't they come for me? I mean, if getting me was the plan all along then leaving me behind doesn't make sense." As I said this all I could think of was how Shane had been nice and too happy all night. Almost as though he'd been celebrating something...like me being abducted.

What an ass.

"I don't know, that's the one part I don't understand." Eli smoothed a hand along his jawline. The scratchy sound of his stubble found its way to my ears. "Maybe the tranquilizer was meant for you, but when they spotted Tate they felt forced to use it on him instead. Could be you never gave them a good time to take you without it."

I reached for a couple of paper plates from the cabinet near the stove and pulled the sandwiches off the heat.

"Maybe," I whispered. "Or it could've been because I didn't get as hammered as everyone else and neither did Ridley."

"Hammered? You were drinking?" There was an edge to his words that sent my stomach somersaulting.

"Shane brought a cooler of beer with him. We were all drinking. I didn't have as much as everyone else, but the guys got smashed. Becca too. Me and Ridley were the only ones who didn't get shitfaced." I found two Styrofoam bowls next to the paper plates and spooned the warm soup into them. "Even though Tate was in the woods I was still worried something might happen, especially after Ridley's warning, so I didn't drink much."

"You got drunk. In the woods. At night. With Shane in your presence." He accentuated his words as though I were a small child being scolded.

I folded my arms across my chest and held his gaze. "No, I didn't get drunk. Tipsy, sort of. It went away after I saw Violet in the woods, though. I was sober most of the night."

Shit, Violet. I'd forgotten all about her.

"Doesn't matter if you were sober. My point is, you drank alcohol in the woods with Shane after everything you know."

"I think it does matter. Not being hammered like everyone else was what saved my ass."

"How did it save you?" Eli growled.

"They probably thought I'd get drunk and fall asleep. I'm sure the tranquilizer was so I'd stay asleep during transport to wherever they planned to take me. Seeing Tate in the woods botched their plan. They were forced to use it on him instead and since I wasn't as drunk as they'd hoped they were forced to leave me. So, yeah. Not being hammered saved me."

Eli didn't speak for a while. Neither of us did. My mind had circled back through the night and all I could think about was Violet.

"What happened to Violet? Did Tate make sure she went home?" I asked.

"No." Eli shook his head. "He never got to say anything to her. He didn't even know she was in the woods last night when I talked to him earlier."

"Didn't you send him a message letting him know that she was?"

"I did, but he was in wolf form while watching you. He didn't get my message until this morning."

"So, he never made sure she got out of the woods safely?"

Eli's eyes lifted to lock with mine. The same level of concern I felt was reflected in them. "No. He didn't."

My heart kick-started inside my chest. "What if she never made it back? What if they decided instead of taking me, they'd take her? Maybe it had nothing to do with me not being drunk enough, maybe they spotted her. A young female wolf. Alone. They'd already taken out Tate. What if they took her, Eli?"

Deep down I already knew the answer to my question. It caused the blood in my veins to run cold.

Violet had been abducted. In my place.

10

"Let's not jump ahead of ourselves," Eli insisted. "First we need to find out if she came home last night."

"And what do we do if she didn't?" I asked. It was time we let his dad know what was going on. Violet was only sixteen. She was a kid.

"We'll figure it out when we cross that bridge," Eli said as he took a bite of his grilled cheese.

I couldn't believe he was eating in a time like this. I wouldn't be able to until I knew whether Violet was safe. "Let's swing by her place and see if she's there."

"Right now. Okay, sure." He dusted his hands off on his shorts, sending buttered crumbs flying through the air, and headed toward his front door. "Let's go see if she's home then."

My heart pounded against my rib cage as I followed after him. Before I reached the door my cell buzzed with a new text. It was from Gracie.

Callie just called me. Violet didn't come home

last night. No one has seen her since yesterday afternoon. I'm going over to sit with her. Gran left to pick Dad up from somewhere, let her know I'm probably spending the night with Callie, okay?

I re-read Gracie's text, focusing on the sentence where she said Violet didn't come home last night. Dizziness swept through me. I gripped Eli's shirt to steady myself.

"What's wrong?" he asked as he paused and glanced over his shoulder at me.

"That was Gracie. Violet didn't come home last night. No one has seen her since yesterday afternoon. She's missing," I whispered.

The floor beneath me spun as my heartbeat continued to thunder in my ears. I released my grip on Eli and thought I might crumble to the floor.

Violet had been abducted. She'd been taken in my place.

Eli shifted to face me. His hand gripped my hips as he pulled me into him. My skin tingled where his hands touched me.

"We still don't know she was taken by Shane and his brothers. We have reason to suspect, don't get me wrong, but we don't know for sure," he insisted.

"Are you kidding me? What more do you need?" I maneuvered my way out of his grasp. Why didn't he just call a spade a spade? We both knew who'd taken her.

Eli ran a hand through his hair. "It's time we take this to my dad. I'm sure Violet's parents have already let him know she's missing but in order to find her as soon as possible he'll need to know everything we do."

A lump formed in my throat. Would we be reprimanded for keeping so much information to ourselves? I forced the thought away before it could truly take hold. It didn't matter. Not now. Violet was missing. Glenn was missing. Who would go missing next if we didn't say something?

"Let's head to my parents' place. We need to tell him before he sends out anyone to search for her." Eli exited through the front door. Thick, humid air wafted inside the trailer. It smothered all the cool air inside, making my skin feel sticky with sweat instantly.

I started through the door behind him, taking my time on the wooden steps because my legs felt like Jell-O since learning Violet was missing. Eli reached for my hand. His fingers intertwined with mine and the familiar rush of electricity I always seemed to feel at his touch flowed across my skin. The sensation rolled over me like a sedative.

Neither of us spoke as we started toward his parent's trailer. Guilt ate at me from not having made sure Violet had gone home after I spotted her in the woods. I could have done something. I was there.

When we were nearly at his parent's front door, Eli glanced at me. His hand squeezed mine. "It's going to be okay. We'll get Violet back. She'll be fine."

"I hope you're right," I said.

I paused once we reached his parent's porch and messaged Gracie back, letting her know I'd tell Gran where she was. I also mentioned how sorry I was to hear about Violet.

"Ready?" Eli asked as he stepped onto their porch.

I shoved my cell into my back pocket and nodded.

Eli rapped his knuckles on the door twice before turning

the knob. I climbed the stairs and stepped in behind him, my body a bundle of nerves.

A shiver slipped through me. The place was like an icebox. Cold air blasted through the vent above where I stood. Eli stepped further into the living room and I followed. My flip-flops slapped against the laminate wood floors as I walked.

"Hey, honey," Eli's mom's soft voice floated to my ears. "To what do we owe the pleasure of this surprise visit to?"

June Vargas was a sweet woman in her mid-fifties who was absolutely stunning. She was short and slender with dark hair down to her waist. It was her bright green eyes each of the Vargas boys had inherited.

"Hey, Mama," Eli said in a voice that sent goose bumps prickling across my skin. He was a mama's boy at heart, I could tell from the way he talked to her, and I thought it was the sweetest thing ever.

"Is that little Mina Ryan behind you?" Mrs. Vargas peeked around Eli to get a better look at me. "How have you been, sugar? That daddy of yours doing okay?"

"Hi, Mrs. Vargas. I've been good. And yeah, Dad is okay." I stepped around Eli so I could see me better. She sat on the couch, folding clothes while the TV played softly in the background. From the few seconds I'd heard, it sounded like a daytime soap opera.

"That's good. What about your grandmother? She doing all right?" Her hands continued to fold laundry as her gaze remained on me.

I nodded and tucked a few strands of hair behind my ear. "She's good."

"That garden of her's still doing good? I thought I saw

your sister out there last week with her. I just love Gracie likes to garden. It's so sweet."

"Gran's garden is her pride and joy. She's out there every chance she gets," I insisted. "And Gracie does like it. She soaks up Gran's knowledge whenever she can."

A wide smile stretched across Mrs. Vargas's face. "That's good. Hobbies are good things to have. They keep people out of trouble." She reached for a fluffy towel and folded it in half. "So, what are the two of you stopping by for?" Her eyes shifted from me to Eli.

"We have something pack related to share with Dad. Is he around?" Eli asked.

"He is. He's in the back bedroom. Let me get him for you." She laid the towel she'd folded on top of the stack beside her and stood to walk toward the back of the trailer. Her footsteps made little noise across the laminate flooring when she started down the hall.

"You can sit down if you want." Eli motioned to a recliner. "I'll do all the talking."

"Okay." I stepped toward the recliner, deciding I had no qualms about him doing all the talking.

"He'll be out in a second. Let him finish up with the call he's on," Mrs. Vargas said as she positioned herself in the same spot on the couch from before and resumed folding clothes. "He's been so busy lately. I don't know what's going on but it must be serious. He's been under a tremendous amount of stress. I'm presuming whatever the two of you have to say is going to add to it, am I right?" Her gaze drifted between the two of us.

"Yeah, but I don't have any choice," Eli said.

"Oh, Lord. I'm not mad at you. All I'm saying is he's been

under a lot of stress lately. I'm hoping everything will mellow out again soon."

"It will. It always does," Eli insisted.

"I know," she sighed. "He's getting too old for this, though. I keep telling him he needs to give the Alpha responsibilities to you. The man needs to retire. He needs a dang break." Her full lips twisted into a frown as the area between her brows creased with worry. "You're old enough to handle everything. Heck, you're a year older than what he was when he took over for his father. He's such a control freak sometimes."

I pretended I was invisible. Never had so much pack information been said in front of me before. Being privy to it felt like I'd invaded their privacy somehow. I forced my eyes to take in the inside of their trailer. It had been years since I'd been inside.

The last time cream-colored wallpaper had decorated the living room walls. I remembered it had tiny blue and pink flowers on it. I wasn't sure if it had come with the trailer or if it had been something Mrs. Vargas had added to give the place a touch of femininity. While I wasn't a fan of wallpaper it had been nice. Now, it was gone, though. Soothing gray walls were in its place. The beige carpet I remembered had been ripped up and replaced by light colored laminate. Even the kitchen cabinets seemed to have undergone a makeover from where I sat. Instead of the dark wood they used to be they'd been painted a smoky blue.

"You've done so much to the place since the last time I was here," I said once I realized everyone had lapsed into silence.

"Thank you," Mrs. Vargas smiled. "It's been a labor of

love for years. We've had the storage shed outside slap full of things Wesley's picked up from carpentry jobs over the years. I finally got him to put some of the items to good use." She finished folding the dishrag she held and stood. "Come look at this bathroom. It's the only room in the house we've completely finished."

I stood and followed her down the narrow hall.

"The last time I was here, I remember the cream-colored wallpaper you had with the blue and pink flowers. This gray looks great, though. I love the color."

"Thank you. I think it makes the whole place look bigger." She swung open the third door on the left. I'd never been this far into the Vargas trailer. In fact, I'd never made it past the kitchen and living room area. "We finished this room couple weekends ago. I don't know if you ever saw it before, but everything in here was a god-awful pink. The sink, the toilet, the bathtub. It looked like somebody vomited all over the darn room."

I wasn't surprised. Some of the trailers Bobby rented out where what some would call vintage. I called them ugly. Thank goodness Gran's trailer hadn't been one of them. It was decent. Not completely updated, but decent.

"This looks great," I said as I took in the small room. The walls had been painted a light coffee color that matched the tile in the shower and the light-colored flooring made the room seem larger than what it was. There was a rustic farmhouse vibe I found appealing. "I love those wire baskets on the wall."

"I found them at a thrift shop in town and painted them myself."

"Crafty,"

Male voices sounded from the living room. Our Alpha seemed to have finished his phone call. Suddenly, I found it hard to breathe.

"Oh, sounds like Wesley finished his call," Mrs. Vargas said as she closed the bathroom door and started back down the hall. I followed after her, my nervousness coming back full force.

"I know I should come by more often." I heard Eli say as we stepped into the living room.

"Dinner once a week with you would be nice," Mr. Vargas insisted as he positioned himself in the recliner I'd been sitting in previously.

I couldn't believe Eli had let me sit in his dad's chair.

Mr. Vargas's eyes bypassed his wife and flicked to me as I stepped to Eli's side. The corners of his lips twisted upward.

"Mina," he greeted me. His rich voice rumbled through the trailer, bouncing off the thin walls and causing my heart to pound ferociously inside my chest. So much power emanated from him. "How have you been?"

"I've been well," I said trying my damnedest to hold his gaze. "Thank you."

"Good, and I presume your family is doing well also?"

"Yes, sir."

Mr. Vargas's eyes shifted back to Eli. "Then what do I owe the pleasure of this visit to?"

Eli cleared his throat. "Have you heard about Violet Marshal?"

"What about her?" From his tone, it was clear he knew something but he wasn't willing to give away any details.

"Did you know she's been missing since yesterday?" Eli asked.

Mr. Vargas nodded. Sadness drooped his expression and weighed down his shoulders. "Yes, her parents came to me early this morning with the news. Do either of you know anything about her disappearance?"

"Unfortunately, we do." Eli scratched the back of his neck while I shifted on my feet. "We have reason to believe there are poachers abducting wolves from the pack."

"What led you to believe this?" he asked.

Eli glanced at me and then back to his father before speaking again. I wasn't sure if he was checking to see if I wanted to tell his dad what I'd found in the woods or if he was making sure I was still breathing. When I barely acknowledged him, he continued talking. "Mina has seen some interesting things in the woods lately. She thought she witnessed Glenn in wolf form running through the woods the night he disappeared. A couple of days later, she stumbled upon an area in the woods that looked as though a struggle had taken place. There was blood on the ground and some scratch marks."

"Did you see the area where a struggle supposedly happened with your own eyes?" Mr. Vargas asked Eli. He wasn't calling me a lair, but instead seemed to be making sure there was a whiteness for what I'd claimed to see all the same.

"I did. Mina brought me to the area later that night. While we were there, we heard a couple of guys—humans—talking about needing to abduct a female wolf. They were making a deal with someone for money in exchange for the wolf."

"And, you think Violet is whom they decided to abduct?" Mr. Vargas asked. "You think someone is targeting our pack for their gain?"

"I do," Eli insisted.

"What proof do you have? I don't mean discredit what you're telling me, but I know from years of experience that when young ones become Moon Kissed they don't always stay with their pack. Sometimes they move on to find new places for themselves and carve their own paths. Others, venture into the woods and become lost, exhilarated by the feel of the change and forget to double back when they've gone too far."

"That's not what happened to Violet." The words propelled themselves passed my lips without thought. I'd promised Eli I would let him do all the talking, but I didn't like the implications being placed on Violet. She hadn't run away to carve a new path for herself. She hadn't ventured into the woods and gotten lost either. "She was taken. I can feel it in my gut."

Mr. Vargas's eyes locked on mine. "While I am generally a firm believer in intuition, I have to say, in this situation I need more proof than that. There are bigger issues I'm dealing with at the moment. Ones that involve the pack as a whole. I don't have the time or the man power to shift my attention to one particular girl who may or may not be truly missing. Same goes with Glenn."

"This isn't just about one particular girl, Father. It's not about Glenn either," Eli insisted. "This involves the pack as a whole. Who's to say the same people won't take another member?"

"I understand your cause for concern, son. I truly do," Mr. Vargas insisted with a nod of his head. "but I cannot push the matter I'm currently dealing with aside to focus on this one. It's of too much importance."

My heart deflated. Coming here had done no good. We had no tangible proof. All we had was what we'd witnessed. Unless Tate had something to add. Maybe he'd seen who shot him with the tranquilizer. Maybe he'd heard something.

"What about Tate? Did you know he was shot with a tranquilizer last night, the same night Violet disappeared?" I asked ready to lay everything on the table. Eli stiffened beside me and I wasn't sure if I was supposed to divulge that information. If I wasn't, it was too late now.

"I've heard nothing of the nature. How do you know this?" Mr. Vargas asked. His intense gaze pinned me in place.

"Eli told me. Tate was watching over me last night while I camped with my boyfriend and some of his friends." I swallowed hard, hating having used the word boyfriend in reference to Alec in front of Eli and the Alpha of the pack. There didn't seem to be a better label to place on him, though. He wasn't a friend. I didn't kiss my friends the way we'd kissed in the lake last night. Yet, he wasn't a boyfriend either. Not really.

I guess I wasn't sure what we were.

"Why would you need my son to watch over you while you camped?" Mr. Vargas asked. It was a valid question.

"One of my boyfriend's friends happens to be one of the guys who abducted Glenn. And since I've been Moon Kissed and am what they're looking for next, Eli figured it would be best to have someone watch over me while I camped."

"Why would you put yourself in such danger? Why spend the night in the woods with them at all?" Mrs. Vargas asked. There was a wild note whirling in the pitch of her voice.

"I wanted more information. I wanted to find out where

Glenn was. If he was alive. Taryn deserves to know what happened to him."

"Did you find anything more out?" Mr. Vargas asked.

"No." I pulled in a deep breath and exhaled slowly. "I did happen to see Violet in the woods, though. She was running in wolf form. Alone. I didn't think it was wise for her to be there, considering what I knew, so I sent a message to Eli. He said he'd message Tate. Unfortunately, Tate was shot with a tranquilizer and passed out. He was never able to help Violet home safely. I was warned by one of the Caraway witches on the camping trip that I needed to be careful that night. She had a gut feeling something was going to happen to me. I think it was Shane and his brothers planning to abduct me."

"You think they took Violet instead of you. Why?" Mr. Vargas asked.

I could feel everyone's eyes boring into me. Unease prickled across my skin.

"She was a weaker target than me," I whispered.

Mr. Vargas seemed to consider what I'd said.

"I think you're right," he said after a few minutes had passed. "Eli, if you wouldn't mind, I'd like to speak to you alone." He stood and walked toward be back of the trailer.

A loud sigh rushed past Mrs. Vargas's lips one they were gone.

"I hope you're wrong. I've been praying all morning that little girl would find her way back home on her own, that maybe she got turned around in the woods or wandered too far," she said. "But now, I can't help thinking you might be right."

"I was hoping I was wrong too."

Mrs. Vargas stood and crossed to where I was so she

could pull me into a hug. "I'm glad you weren't taken, Mina. I know it's sad Violet was, but if it had been you...I don't know what Eli would have done. He would be beside himself if something ever happened to you."

My breath hitched in my throat as I awkwardly returned her hug. Did she really think Eli cared for me that much?

"My heart is breaking to pieces for Violet's family," she insisted as tears glistened in her eyes. "I couldn't imagine."

Silence built between us as we both became lost in our thoughts.

"How rude of me. Can I get you anything to drink? I'm not sure how long they'll be talking for," Mrs. Vargas said.

I shook my head. "I'm okay."

"Well then, at least have a seat. You're making me nervous standing there."

I crossed the room and sat at the end of the couch opposite her. It didn't feel right sitting in the recliner now that I knew it was the Alpha's seat.

From the corner of my eye, I noticed Mrs. Vargas had gone back to folding laundry. Her attention zeroed in on the couple arguing on TV. I caught the tail end of the dramatic scene. They seemed to be fighting over something that involved the woman's younger sister.

"I can't believe Scarlett did that. Now her husband knows she knows. I've been waiting for five episodes to find out when that all would come out," Mrs. Vargas said. She'd somehow managed to submerge herself in her show after everything we'd just talked about.

When Eli and his dad came back I was ready to get out of there. I'd listened to all of the soap opera drama I cared to.

"You ready?" Eli asked. Tension swirled through his

green eyes. It had me guessing the conversation with his dad might not have gone well.

"Yeah, sure."

"I'm glad you stopped by, Mina," Mrs. Vargas called out to me as I followed Eli toward the door. "Swing by anytime. It's always a pleasure to have you over. Oh, and tell your grandma I said hello."

"I will, thank you."

"And, Eli," she lifted her voice, giving it a motherly tone. "You better stop being so scarce around this place. We would love to see you more, especially the boys. You know how much they all adore you."

"I know," Eli said. His cheeks tinted pink and I had to hide my grin. "I'll try to swing by at least once a week for dinner."

"You know, you could also offer to let us take a gander at your place. I know I speak for all of us when I say we'd love to see what you've done on the inside," Mr. Vargas chimed in.

"I will." Eli gripped the handle to the front door and twisted. Once we were outside he glared at me. "What are you smirking at?" The corners of his lips twisted into the ghost of a smile, letting me know he wasn't as irritated with me as he pretended to be.

"I told you to stop by your parents for dinner once a week, didn't I? You should have listened to me," I said as I nudged him with my elbow.

"That you did."

My cell buzzed in my back pocket with the new text as we headed toward his place. It was Gracie again.

Can you take Winston for a walk, please?

I rolled my eyes and let out a puff of air. How had I

known I'd end up being the one to take care of that stupid puppy? And, Winston? When had she named him?

"What's wrong?" Eli asked.

"I have to swing by my place to take Gracie's puppy for a walk," I sighed. "I'll come to yours when I'm done."

"Oh, so you do still want to have dinner with me tonight?" A satisfied look glimmered in his eyes.

"Actually, I wanted to hear what your dad said. You looked irritated when you came back from talking with him."

Eli crammed his hands into his front pockets. "And here I thought you were all about enjoying my company tonight."

I shoved him playfully. "Will you stop. We have serious matters talk about, and don't think you're getting out of keeping me in the loop on it. Whatever it is, I want to know." Even if it went against his father's orders.

Pack law was pack law, though. When the Alpha said it couldn't be repeated, that was it. Mum was the word.

"Get the dog. We'll take it for a walk together. I'll fill you in on everything then," Eli insisted, surprising me.

"Okay." I darted up the stairs to my place, eager to get the little runt so Eli could tell me everything his dad had said.

11

Eli grabbed the leash from me after a few steps. I wasn't sure if he thought I wasn't walking the puppy right or if he just wanted to do it himself. I didn't care either way. Having to stop every two seconds to untangle myself from its leash was getting on my nerves. A low chuckle rumbled from him. I glanced at him to see a wide smile building across his face while he watched Winston sniff everything in his path.

"I didn't know you were a dog lover," I teased him.

His bright green eyes sucked me in when he shifted to glance at me.

"Who isn't a dog lover?" he asked.

"Me for one. I've never been much of an animal lover."

"Says the girl who's a wolf."

"That's different," I insisted as I tucked a few stray hairs behind my ear.

"How? A wolf is an animal, isn't it?"

"Yeah, but I change into one I don't have to babysit it."

"There are some in the pack who would disagree with that statement. They happen to think wearing silver is how we babysit our wolf."

"Hmmm...I never thought of it that way," I said.

"Sort of makes sense though, doesn't it?"

"Yeah."

Silver was how we controlled our wolf self throughout the month. I'd often thought of it as a way to keep a leash on our wolves, but I'd never thought of it as a way to babysit it.

We continued down the gravel road that wove through the trailer park, allowing Winston to sniff and run as much as he saw fit. Sylvie Hess stood outside her place when we neared it. She was blowing bubbles with her youngest boy. Her face lit up when she saw us.

"Aw, you two are so precious together," she gushed. "I love that you're taking a stroll with your puppy. How sweet."

Her words made unease snake through my stomach. How had I been blind to what we might look like while walking a dog together? Shit. Now everyone who saw us would probably think we were a couple. I would never hear the end of it

"It's Gracie's dog. She's at Callie's helping to console her. I'm taking him for a walk for her and Eli just happened to join," I said to clarify.

"Right," Sylvie said dragging the word out.

My teeth sank into my lower lip. She didn't believe me. No matter what I said it wouldn't change her view of the situation. Why did this bother me so much? I shouldn't care what Sylvie or anyone thought in regards to Eli and me. It wasn't their business.

Only, I did care.

I grabbed the leash from Eli and continued walking,

making sure to keep my head high and my face in a relaxed expression. Once we were out of Sylvie's earshot I slowed my pace. Eli needed to catch up to me and we needed to talk about the conversation he'd had with his dad. No more chitchat.

"I didn't think someone assuming we were a couple would offend you so much. Damn," Eli said. He smoothed a hand along the back of his neck as he exhaled a long breath. Instantly, I felt horrible for the way I'd overreacted. "That was harsh. Even for you."

I closed my eyes and pulled in a deep breath. "I know. I'm sorry. I just don't want people thinking we're together."

"Why?"

I couldn't answer him because I didn't know the answer myself.

"What was it your dad said to you earlier?" I asked ignoring his question and skipping to one of my own.

I could feel Eli's eyes on me. His gaze grew hard and cold. I knew I'd pissed him off by sidestepping his question, but I didn't care.

"He's leaving the situation to me to handle."

My brows furrowed. "Why?"

"Why not? You don't think I'm capable?"

Great, just when I thought it wasn't possible to make him anymore upset with me I go and question his ability to handle the situation on his own.

"It's not that. I think you're more than capable, but I also think it's a big task to take on alone. What does your dad have going on that's so important he can't handle the situation himself?"

"You know I can't tell you that," Eli insisted. "It's Alpha

business. All I can do is reiterate what you heard my mom say earlier. It's something big. I know it sounds like he doesn't care about what's going on, but trust me, he has the packs well-being at mind right now." There was a pleading tone that registered in Eli's voice that had me second-guessing my irritation toward his dad. Maybe I should give him the benefit of the doubt. After all, he hadn't ever done our pack wrong before. Westley Vargas took his position as Alpha very seriously.

I did hope that he made an announcement once whatever it was he'd been dealing with had been handled. Curiosity would get the best of me otherwise.

"Okay. Fine." I locked eyes with him. "I won't ask again and I'll trust that your dad has the pack's best interest at heart like always. Also, I think you'll handle this situation just fine without him."

"Thanks for the vote of confidence." Eli pulled a scrap of paper from his pocket. "Dad did give me this, though. It's a number for a contact at the station."

"A contact at the station? The police station?"

"Yeah." Eli passed the scrap of paper to me.

I read off the number. It wasn't familiar. The name at the top said Dan, but there wasn't a last name. While I wasn't familiar with many of the police officers in town, I did know one thing they all had in common.

"Why would your dad have a contact at the station? I thought everyone at the police station was human."

"They are." Eli nodded. "Apparently, this guy and my dad were friends when they were in high school. A group of trouble-making vampires came through town, searching for the Montevallo family. This guy, Dan, got mixed in with some of them by accident one night and my dad was forced to shift in front of him to save his life. Since then Dan has done anything he can to make sure the pack has a smooth stay here in Mirror Lake because of it. He's been helping the pack for years with things. He's like our intel at the station. When something strange happens that doesn't seem it can be explained rationally, he reaches out to dad to see if there's something supernatural going on. The guy is legit."

"I didn't realize we had someone on the inside like that."

Winston paused to pee on Felicia's flowers at the edge of her trailer. I pulled on his leash, making him start walking again so he wouldn't take a dump there too.

"Dad has mentioned his name a couple times, but I never knew the full story behind their friendship until today."

"Isn't your dad nervous Dan might tell our secret to someone?" I had to ask. The fear was front and center in my mind.

"Nah. Dan's kept the secret for this long, I don't see why he would tell anyone. Besides, who would believe him?"

"Good point," I said. "So, what can Dan do to help with this situation? I don't understand why your dad gave you his number."

"Dad thinks the same thing I do—Violet wouldn't have been sent directly to whoever is in charge. Shane's brother would have to call and arrange a meeting with whoever is running the thing so they could do an exchange. Violet has to be held somewhere while all the details are being worked out. What better place than that guy's own house?"

"So, you're going to call this Dan guy and see if he can get you Shane's brother's addresses?"

"Exactly."

"That's a good idea."

"I thought so too," Eli grinned.

We passed Taryn and Glenn's tiny trailer. Glenn's truck still sat in the same spot as the night he disappeared, but Taryn's cherry red car was gone. I wondered where she was. At work? Searching for Glenn? At a doctor's appointment? My chest squeezed at the thought of her raising her baby without him. While I knew she wouldn't be the first in the pack to raise a child alone her situation was a hell of a lot sadder than anyone else's.

"Give me a second, I'm gonna run inside and grab my cell. I'd like to give Dan a call. It's time we get this ball rolling," Eli said once we neared his trailer.

"Okay." I paused, bringing Winston to a stop with me. He glanced at me. "Just stopping for a second," I whispered. He seemed content enough with my answer and moved to sniff a large grease spot on the gravel. I tugged on his leash, detouring him from it. He decided to try and follow after Eli instead.

"Don't let him piss on my steps," Eli grumbled when he noticed Winston hot on his heals.

"I thought you were a dog lover. Why do you sound so harsh?" I chuckled.

"Funny," Eli muttered before he disappeared inside.

I watched Winston strut around while I waited for Eli to come back. A black beetle caught his attention and I laughed when he pawed at it like a cat, jumping back each time it moved toward him. He was a cute little thing. I could see why Gracie was so infatuated with him. Thinking of her had me glancing at the Marshal's trailer. From where I stood I couldn't tell if there were any lights on, but the vehicles parked in the driveway let me know everyone was home. Guilt ripped through my chest. The desire to walk over and tell Violet's parents everything I knew was nearly overwhelming.

Would it do any good, though?

Eli's door opened and he crept down the steps with his cell in hand. He glanced at the slip of paper his dad had given him and punched in Dan's number. I could hear the phone ring from where I stood. Eli took a few steps away for privacy. I watched Winston attack the bug while trying not to appear as though I was eavesdropping. Eli's one-sided conversation floated to my ears, but I couldn't make much out. I did hear him give Shane and his brother's first and last names to Dan, though. Seconds later he hung up and started to where I stood.

"Dan is on it. He said to give them about twenty minutes," Eli said. He took Winston's leash from me and I let him.

"That's fast." Twenty minutes didn't seem long at all.

"Yeah, Dan doesn't seem to mess around. He seems to be strictly business."

"Which is a good thing."

Eli nodded as we started toward my place. Gran pulled up in my dad's truck before we reached the porch. She looked tiny behind the giant steering wheel. And pissed. I glanced at Dad in the passenger seat. His face was pressed against the window and he was drooling while he slept.

"Hey, Gran," I called to her as she slipped out of Dad's truck. "Let me help you."

"I've got it. I got him in here all by myself and I can get him out," she grumbled.

"Where did you pick him up at?" I ignored what she'd said and rounded the passenger side to offer assistance.

"Eddie's bar," Gran muttered. She opened the passenger door and had to catch Dad before he fell out. "He's as drunk as a darn skunk."

When wasn't he? He'd been this way for years now.

"One of these days his liver is going give out on him." She maneuvered his dead weight around, but seemed as though she was having a hard time. I stepped in to help. "A person can't pump their body full of poison the way he does and not expect it to have consequences."

Dad slurred something I couldn't make out as I lifted one of his arms over my shoulder. Both Gran and I stumbled under his weight, but Eli was there to catch us. He'd tied Winston to the porch. I was glad. There was no way Gran and I could carry Dad in the trailer by ourselves when he was this wasted.

It didn't take long for Eli to get Dad situated in his bed. Afterward, we brought in the groceries Gran had bought.

"Oh, Gracie wanted me to tell you she's staying at Callie's tonight. Did you hear about Violet?" I asked as I started to put away some of the groceries.

Gran's face darkened. "I did. That's why I went to the store on my way to pick your dad up. I wanted to make them a casserole so they don't have to worry about cooking. My heart goes out to them. I've been praying all day Violet would make it home safely on her own." Gran placed her cold ingredients in the refrigerator and then shifted a look at me. "I don't have a good feeling about this, though."

A shiver ran along my spine. Intuition was my grandmother's best friend. I often thought if she hadn't been born into the world of werewolves she would've been born into the world of witches. Some days it seemed as though she walked between both worlds, tiptoeing along the line. While many in the pack thought of her as a healer, I saw her as more than that. Gran was a healer with a vast knowledge of herbs and remedies, but she also had kickass intuition. She'd taught me intuition was something to listen to. It wasn't something to be ignored.

"What do you mean?" I asked her.

"I think there's something suspicious going on. That little girl didn't run off on her own and get lost. She's either hurt or someone's taken her."

I couldn't believe how spot on she was. My gaze drifted to Eli. He stood near the front door, leaning against the wall. Astonishment flashed through his eyes. I couldn't remember a time when he'd ever witnessed Gran's intuition at work. In fact, I didn't know if he knew it existed.

I guess we were both learning things about each other's family today. One secret for another.

"I hope I'm wrong, but the feeling is strong. I think something dark happened to that poor girl and it's going to tear her family apart if she isn't found soon," Gran insisted as she went back to putting away groceries.

I wanted to tell her how right she was, but knew I couldn't.

"I will say, though," Gran said. "I'm surprised to see the two of you hanging out so much lately." Her eyes shifted from me to Eli and then back to me again. One of her brows lifted and I knew what she was thinking. The same thing Sylvie Hess had—that we were a couple now.

What was with everyone always pushing us to be together?

"It isn't what you're thinking," I insisted.

Eli cleared his throat. "I should probably get going. I'll see you later, Mina." He bent down to pet Winston who had curled up at his feet and then cracked the front door and slipped out.

"Eli, wait," I muttered. Guilt gnawed at my insides from spastically having corrected yet another person about us. I was sure he thought I sounded as though being with him was the most horrible thing on the planet.

I dashed to the door and down the stairs after him.

"Eli, wait!" I shouted. He paused in the gravel road. "I didn't mean it the way it sounded," I insisted once I reached his side.

"It's okay. No harm, no foul." He shrugged. "I'll let you know when Dan gets me an address." He started walking again. I followed, unable to let the situation go so easily. I felt horrible.

The last thing I wanted to do was hurt him. It was more than that though. The strange pull I felt toward him wouldn't allow things to end on weird terms between us tonight.

"What about my grilled cheese and tomato soup? Don't I get to finish it?" I asked, grasping at straws. It was all I had.

Eli cocked his head to the side and glanced at me. The sliver of a smirk twisted at the corners of his lips. "Of course."

Tension dissolved from my muscles and I released a breath as we continued toward this trailer. Once we stepped inside, Eli warmed up my grilled cheese and soup in the microwave. He placed it in front of me on the counter and motioned for me to eat.

I took a bite from my sandwich and realized his eyes were still on me. "Don't watch me eat. It's creepy."

"I just wanted to make sure it was warm enough for you. That microwave can be fickle."

I gave him a thumbs up. "It's warm."

"Good," he said as he warmed up his food next.

My cell buzzed from in my back pocket when I went to take another bite of my sandwich. I pulled it out, thinking it was Gracie. It wasn't. Alec was calling me.

He couldn't have called at a worse time. I'd just smoothed things over with Eli, but I couldn't ignore his call.

"I'm going to take this outside. I'll be right back," I said as I started toward the door.

"Everything okay?"

"Yeah, everything's fine. Give me one second," I said as I opened the front door and stepped down the wooden stairs.

I swiped my thumb across the screen to answer Alec's call. "Hey, what's up?"

"How are you feeling today?" he asked. His voice rumbled through the phone in a low tone, making him sound as though he'd just woken up.

"I'm fine. I think the question is how are *you* feeling today?" I countered.

I knew he'd woken with a hangover from hell this morning. It was why I'd offered to walk home instead of having him drive me.

"Better now. I felt like death this morning, though. Thanks for walking. Made me feel like a jerk letting you, but I'm glad you did. I came home and slept for hours. I woke up about fifteen minutes ago and ate something."

"Do you feel human yet?"

"Yeah, finally." The sound of him drinking something filtered through the phone. "Do you want to go to the movies tonight? Everyone wants to see some new thriller."

"The remake of that eighties movie?" I'd been dying to see it, but hadn't been able to make the time.

"That's the one. It starts at nine. Think you can come? I can swing by and pick you up," he said before taking another swig of his drink.

I wanted to go, but I didn't think it was a good idea. The timing was bad. Eli was waiting on Dan to call with the address is for Shane's brothers and I had a feeling once he got them we'd be making a trip to their houses tonight. If I was out with Alec, Eli would go alone.

There was not a chance in hell I was letting that happen.

"I wish I could, but I can't tonight. I promised Gracie I'd stay home and watch movies with her." The lie rolled off my tongue easily.

I wasn't sure when, but at some point, lying to Alec had become normal. It had to say something about our relationship. Maybe it said something about me too.

"Oh, okay. Talk to you tomorrow then," Alec said. He didn't sound pissed, just disappointed.

"I'm sorry, but I really need to spend time with my sister tonight. She's been feeling down lately," I said without knowing where I was going with the excuse. All I knew was I needed a legitimate reason. One he'd understand. One that didn't leave our relationship in jeopardy. I liked Alec. More than he knew. He was part of my before. He spoke to the human side of me. A side I wanted to keep alive and strong. "Her best friend's sister ran away. It's got her feeling a little shaken up."

It wasn't the entire truth, but it was as close as I could get.

"Really? That's horrible. Yeah, sure. I understand. Spend time with her. Maybe we can hang out sometime tomorrow?"

God, he was so damn sweet. He could do so much better than me. Part of me thought maybe it was time I let him go.

"Thanks for understanding," I said meaning it. "I'll give you a call tomorrow sometime, okay? Tell me how the movie goes."

"Sure."

"I'd better get in there and make some popcorn. Have fun tonight." I hated how strong my desire to get off the phone with him was. It had me feeling like a horrible person. Deep down I knew I wasn't, things were just complicated. "I'll talk to you tomorrow."

"Yeah, tomorrow. Have a good night," Alec said.

"Bye," I said before I hung up.

I crammed my phone into my back pocket and started up the steps to Eli's door as I smoothed my hands over my face. Flickers of guilt spread through me like a wildfire, but I tried to stomp them out. Telling Alec the lie and spending time with Eli tonight instead had everything to do with the pack and nothing else. I had to help get Violet back. After all, I was partially responsible for her being missing.

Eli was on the phone when I stepped inside. He jotted down something on a scrap of paper. I hoped it was the addresses for Shane's older brothers. I closed the door behind me and crossed to where he stood at the kitchen counter. His handwriting was horrible, nothing better than chicken scratch, but I was able to make out two addresses.

"Okay, yeah. Thanks, Dan," Eli said before hanging up.

He pushed the scrap of paper toward me. "There we go. We now have Peter and Drew's addresses."

"Is that what that says?" I squinted as I glared at the paper, giving him a hard time. "I don't read chicken scratch well."

"What are you taking about? My handwriting is perfect. A little on the small side, but perfect nonetheless. Maybe you need glasses?"

"Ha, ha." I shoved him playfully. "I don't need glasses. You need handwriting lessons."

"Whatever. Here are the addresses." He picked up the scrap paper. "One lives on Beacon Road and the other on Wilmont Avenue."

"Those are far away from each other, but at least they're in town."

"Yeah. It shouldn't be too hard to find both." Eli grabbed his grilled cheese and shoved it in his mouth. "Which one do you want to start with first?"

"I don't know. I think Peter is most likely to have Glenn, but I think Drew will have Violet."

"We should probably make Violet a top priority since she's younger. Plus, we need to make sure we can get to her before Drew sells her to whoever the boss man is he's working with. She can't be moved again."

"Looks like we're going to Drew's house first then. If Violet isn't there, maybe we'll at least find clues as to where the meeting with the boss was held at."

"Sounds like a plan," Eli said. He motioned to my grilled cheese and tomato soup. "Eat. You're not going to do me any good if you pass out from hunger during the middle of our mission. Hungry ninjas are clumsy ninjas."

"You should totally make a T-shirt with that on it. I'd buy it," I chuckled as I reached for my sandwich. I tore off a corner and dipped it in my soup before popping into my mouth. It was cold, but still tasted good.

"I bet I could sell the heck out of them," Eli grinned.

We ate as quickly as we could. While sustenance was important, so was finding Violet.

"Who called you? Is everything okay with Gracie?" Eli asked. My stomach twisted. I'd hoped he wouldn't ask.

"It was Alec," I said around a mouthful of grilled cheese. There was no point in lying to him. He'd be able to tell. He always had. "He wanted to know if I wanted to go to the movies with him and his friends tonight."

"What did you tell him?"

"That I was watching movies with Gracie tonight. I said her best friend's sister ran away and she was shaken up about it."

Eli froze mid-chew. "You told him what?"

"I had to give him a valid excuse," I insisted hoping he'd understand.

"You can't tell him anything else." Eli's eyes hardened.

"I know," I said, holding his stare.

"Finish eating and then go change into all-black. Do you have something to wear or do you want to borrow a shirt of mine again?"

"If I go home, Gran will want to know what I'm doing. I think it would be best if I borrowed a shirt of yours again. If you don't mind." It was part truth, part lie. Gran would wonder what I was doing, but there was also a part of me that wanted to be submerged in Eli's scent again.

"I'll get you something to wear," Eli said before throwing his trash away.

The conversation about Alec was done. We were back to pack business and I was grateful. I watched him head down the hall as I finished the rest of my sandwich trying not to think about what I was getting myself into by going with Eli to Drew's tonight.

12

Eli's scent surrounded me as I pulled the black T-shirt he'd loaned me to wear over my head. I loved the way he smelled. There was something woodsy yet masculine about his scent. Was it his soap? I closed my eyes and breathed in. The churning of anxiety that had been rolling through my stomach subsided.

I loosened my hair from its hair tie only to pull it up into a high bun again on top of my head. My eyes scanned over myself in Eli's bathroom mirror. Was I ready for this? Could I handle myself out there tonight or would I become a liability if things got tough? My teeth sank into my bottom lip.

Eli was depending on me to stand strong. I had no choice other than to handle my own. We had to rescue Violet.

A soft knock sounded at the bathroom door.

"You ready?" Eli asked. His voice was low and sweet. I knew he wasn't trying to rush me.

"Yeah," I said. "I'm as ready as I will ever be."

I reached for the doorknob and swung the door open. Eli

was close. Too close. He'd been leaning against the doorframe when he knocked. He took a step back and folded his arms across his chest.

"You don't have to come." The area between his brows puckered. I wasn't sure if it was because he preferred I didn't or if it was because of something else. "I can handle this on my own."

"Great. Good to know you can do it without me," I grumbled sarcastically as I passed him and started down the narrow hallway.

"That's not what I meant," Eli said. He was hot on my heels. "All I'm saying is you don't have to come if you don't want to. I can go alone. I'm okay with that."

I glanced over my shoulder and flashed him a nasty look. "Are you trying to tell me I don't have to go if I'm too scared?"

"Well...yeah." His green eyes softened.

Oh, he was heading into dangerous territory.

"I'm not scared." I snapped and then bee-lined for his kitchen to grab a plastic cup from his cabinet. It crinkled in my hand as I gripped too tight while filling it with tap water. My nerves had shifted to rage. How dare he try to leave me behind. "Besides, Violet has a better chance if two of us come to her rescue instead of one."

"I agree."

"Good. Let's get on the road, then." I took another swig of water and managed to catch sight of the smirk shifting across his face. Warmth bloomed through my lower stomach. "What?" I asked as I set my cup on the counter and held his gaze.

"Nothing." He swiped his keys off the counter and started to the front door. He paused once he'd opened it and glanced back at me with that same shit-eating grin plastered on his face. "After you."

I stepped toward him. Sticky warm air blasted across my skin. The sun had gone down hours ago, but it hadn't taken its heat with it.

"Do you have enough gas in your truck?" I asked once I reached the bottom step.

"Yeah." Eli shut the door to his trailer behind him, without locking it started down the steps.

No one ever locked their trailers here. Break-ins were rare in Mirror Lake Trailer Park. Those of us who lived here were respectful of others. We were a tight community. Those who didn't live within the park wouldn't dare rob one of us for a fear of what might happen to them, considering the rumors about us always floating around.

I started around Eli's truck, making my way to the passenger side. Eli climbed behind the steering wheel and wasted no time cranking the engine. It roared to life without trouble.

"All right, let's head to Wilmont Avenue," Eli said as he shifted into reverse and backed out of his driveway.

I stared out the passenger window trying to calm the frantic racing of my heart. It felt as though it might explode. I reached out and turned up the volume on the radio, hoping to drown out the sound of its erratic rhythm and my incessant thoughts. An oldies song I recognized drifted through the stuffy cab. It was one my mom used to sing.

An image of her standing in our kitchen, washing dishes by hand while moving her hips to the beat, flickered through my head. She knew all the words and wasn't half bad at singing either. The memory had my heart settling into a steady beat and the corners of my lips twisting into the ghost of a smile.

God, I missed her sometimes.

I leaned my head against the seat and listened to the lyrics of the song while gazing at the star-speckled sky through the passenger window. The stars blurred together as Eli continued toward Wilmont Avenue.

Roughly thirty minutes passed before we came to the street we were looking for. During that time, I somehow had found a mellow state of zen. Once Eli turned onto Wilmont Avenue all of my zen disappeared. My mouth grew dry and my hands became clammy. We were minutes away from stepping onto enemy grounds.

Anything could happen.

I wiped my palms across my shorts and leaned forward in my seat, searching for the house number Eli had mentioned earlier.

"Is that it right there?" Eli asked. He leaned over the steering wheel, his eyes squinting like an old man's.

"Can you not see that far?"

"I can. I'm just double checking." He came to a slow creep. "Tell me if it's the right number," he said as he passed me the scrap of paper he'd wrote Drew's address on.

"If you can't see that far, I'm scared to be riding in this vehicle with you," I said as I glanced at the scrap of paper. The numbers on the mailbox were a perfect match. "Yup, that's the place."

A shiver slipped up my spine. We were in the middle of nowhere. Nothing surrounded us except miles of woods in every direction.

This place would be a great for werewolves to run...or for someone to hide them.

"I'm going to find somewhere to pull over and park that's out of the way. Then we'll walk to Drew's." Eli insisted as he passed his driveway.

I didn't object. It seemed like a solid plan. In movies, that's what people did when they were trying to be inconspicuous. They didn't pull up to the house and hop out ready to kick ass, they played it safe.

I was totally okay with playing it safe, given the situation.

"Right there might be good." I pointed to a dirt road with a semi-circle off to the side. It looked like a great place to do doughnuts. From the circle tracks across its surface, it seemed as though somebody had practiced theirs recently.

"Perfect," Eli said as he cut a right onto the dirt road. "Good eye."

"Thank you."

Eli killed the engine of his truck and switched the headlights off. I heard him exhale a long breath before he reached for the handle on his door. "Let's do this." He popped the driver side door open and slipped out. "Go ahead and strip."

I swung my gaze around meet his. "Excuse me?"

"You heard me," he said as the wiry hint of a smile curled at the corners of his lips. "I said to go ahead and strip. Did you think we'd be walking up to Drew's house without shifting first?"

My cheeks heated. "Oh. Right. That might not be the smartest thing."

In wolf form, we would have better vision and hearing, plus more speed. We would also be able to pick up Violet and Glenn's scent.

A thought occurred to me as I reached for the handle of the passenger door.

"Why did you have me wear black then? What I was wearing before would've been fine if we were going to shift once we got here anyway."

"Maybe I wanted my scent on you." Eli's words pulled the breath from my lungs and forced my gaze to him again.

Was he serious? My throat grew dry as his lips hooked into a half grin barely visible. I licked my lips and climbed out of his truck, pretending I hadn't heard him.

I reached for the edges of the T-shirt he'd loaned me and lifted it over my head. The heat of his gaze skimmed along the bare skin of my abdomen as soon as I shed the shirt. Butterflies burst into flight through my lower stomach and I found myself fighting against the desire to cover myself. I liked my body, that wasn't the issue, the issue was the way Eli's gaze felt across my skin. It made me tremble in reaction. My bones melted and tiny flickers of lust began to spark through my system.

All of which was inappropriate given the nature of our current situation.

I swallowed hard, ignoring every sensation his stare had awoken within my body and unbuttoned my shorts. Eli's gaze remained on me as I shimmied out of them. When I reached around to unhook my bra, I risked a glance at him. He watched me with a hungry gaze that sent lust sweeping through me. When his tongue moistened his lips as he continued to stare, I thought he might make a move toward me. Part of me wanted him to. It begged for it. The sexual tension rippling off him in waves was mind-numbing, but I refused to give in.

"This isn't a striptease show for you," I said with more attitude laced through my words than I felt.

He cleared his throat. "Sorry."

His gaze drifted to the bench seat of his truck as his fingers fumbled with the brass button on his jeans. The sound of his zipper echoed through the cab. It had my heart pounding a thousand times harder than it should. I forced myself to look away, to look anywhere besides him. The dark section of woods in front of his truck became very interesting as my fingers fumbled with the hook on my bra. Once I managed to get it undone, I tossed it onto my pile of clothes and removed my panties. My silver jewelry came next.

I didn't wait for Eli to say anything about shifting. Instead, I gave in to the change the only way I knew how—by closing my eyes, lifting my head to the sky, and taking slow breaths while thinking of my beautiful wolf. I could picture her in my mind. Her big hazel eyes. Her soft, fluffy fur. Her tiny stature, but fierce spirit.

She was my exact match.

I called out to her with my mind, willing her to come to me when she was ready. Unlike the movies portrayed this moment, there was no painful shifting of bones or grotesque popping noises. There was no sensation of muscles and joints fusing together.

The change was pure magic.

The air around me warmed; the old wolf magick coming to the surface. It blew across my skin, ruffling my hair and sending it flying from my bun. A smile spread across my face as I lifted my arms high above my head. Strands of hair tickled my nose, but I ignored them. Instead, I waited for my wolf to come to me. When a chill slipped along my spine and goose bumps sprouted across my bare skin I knew the goddess of the moon was near. Her magick danced through the air, calling to the wolf inside me. My wolf howled softly in response to her. It was a beautiful noise.

Lightness and loving warmth ignited through my veins as the change intensified. The sensations spread throughout me until an overall sense of weightlessness became all I could feel.

I was air. I was light as a feather. I was free.

Pure love flooded my mind as the cold touch of the Moon Goddess disappeared from my spine to be replaced by an embrace from my wolf. Warmth and the sensation of being grounded and one with the earth trickled through my extremities.

We were one, my wolf and I.

The sounds of the night serenaded me to the present and I made my way around Eli's truck, searching for him. His presence was strong. It pulsed within my veins, calling to me in an unexplainable way. Comfort washed over me once I spotted him. My wolf felt a special connection with Eli, too. She understood he was one from her pack and his ranking, but he was also something more. Whatever it was, it rested just beneath the surface of everything within me.

Eli stepped closer in his wolf form, his familiar green eyes locked with mine. His snout nuzzled my neck and a rush of warmth swept through me from the gesture. The intimacy he was showing caught me off guard. I wasn't sure how I was supposed to react, so I let my wolf do what she wanted. She pressed against him, returning the nuzzle. Seeming satisfied, Eli stepped back and started toward the road. I followed after him, heading straight for Drew's house.

13

I stayed close to Eli as we worked our way up the gravel driveway. My gaze drifted to the woods every other step, searching for threats that might lurk there. Remain alert. It's what my wolf wanted me to do.

When Drew's house came into view I hunkered down low while I continued walking. My gaze swept over the house as we grew closer. It was falling apart and older than I'd imagined. White paint chipped away from it in places and sections of rotted wood ran along the porch. A bloated gutter filled with debris hung at an odd angle along the roof line and the porch was small. A worn porch swing and a pair of muddy work boots were the only things occupying the space. Was Drew the type who made people take their shoes off before stepping inside?

I had a hard time believing so due to the rundown condition of the place.

Lights were on inside and the sound of a TV blaring

filtered through the screen door, but I paid it no mind. Instead, I scooped out the surrounding area.

The house was situated on a large piece of wooded property with no neighbors in either direction. This was good and bad. It made the house a perfect place to hide someone you'd kidnapped, but it also made it hard for anyone to hear their cries for help. It was too secluded.

Eli disappeared around the side of the house and I followed. I wasn't sure what strategy he wanted to apply to the situation—we probably should have discussed things in depth before shifting—but I was willing to roll with whatever he chose. It was too late to do anything else now.

There was nothing along this stretch of the house besides dark windows, a rake propped against the place, and a dry-rotted garden hose tossed haphazardly in the yard. Weeds of various heights and overgrown bushes made it hard to see if there were any basement windows. There didn't appear to be a cellar door either.

However, there was a small shed when we rounded the corner to the back of the house.

Eli crept toward it without me having to suggest we check it out. It must be a new addition to the property because it was in a better shape than the rest of house.

Eli sniffed at the ground, searching for a scent from one of our pack members. I bent my head and did the same, putting all my faith in my wolf's abilities.

Nothing.

Eli must have found the same, because he started back to the house seconds later. The part of me that had hoped we'd be able to find them both without having to step inside the house deflated. I wasn't sure what I'd been thinking. Of course it wouldn't be that easy.

When we rounded to the other side of the house the screen door at the front squeaked open and then banged shut.

Drew had stepped outside.

I hunkered down lower, hoping to blend in with the shadows as I strained my ears to listen to where he was in relation to me. Had he spotted us? I didn't see how. Unless he had game cameras set up. Lots of hunters had them set up around their properties.

I wished we'd thought of that before.

My heart pounded as all the horrible ways this moment could play out circled through my head. Were we about to get shot?

"Yeah, well like I said, I've been trying to get a hold of you all damn day," Drew's voice filtered through the humid air, floating straight to my ears. He was on the phone with someone. From the sound of it, he wasn't happy with whoever he was speaking to. Not only that, but he sounded drunk. His words slurred together the way my fathers did after he'd downed his seventh beer. "Sorry. I know. I'm just pissed. You said you wanted one, and I got it. I can't keep this thing lying around my house forever. It's creepy as hell knowing it's here."

Thing? Was he talking about—Violet? She wasn't a thing.

My lips curled as a low growl built in my throat. Violet was a member of my pack. She was a sixteen-year-old girl he'd abducted not a *thing*.

Eli nudge me from the side. His eyes told me I needed to calm myself. I sighed, but reined myself in as best I could.

"I can meet you whenever," Drew slurred. "I hoped we

would tonight but it ain't happening, is it? Fine. Pick the place and time then."

I shifted around on my paws as a lightness built in my chest. Violet was still here. She hadn't been sold yet.

"Tomorrow night works. Yeah. I'll be there," Drew muttered. "I'll remember. I haven't had that many. I'm fine. I won't forget." His words were drawn-out, weighted down by alcohol and irritation.

I held my breath, hoping he would repeat the place and time for whoever he was on the phone with, but he never did.

"Yeah, yeah. Whatever," Drew muttered before the sound of the screen door swinging open again cut through the night. It slammed shut behind him as he entered the house.

A light flicked on close to where Eli and I were, illuminating the window above us. It was cracked a few inches which allowed us the pleasure of hearing Drew fart while peeing. Eli started forward again and I followed, wondering what he planned to do now. Impatience burned through my veins. I wanted to get Violet now. She was here. We needed to grab her and go.

The tiny porch came into view as we rounded the front of the house. Eli made his way up the rickety steps and headed for the door. I froze. What was he thinking? He couldn't open that door. Not in wolf form.

I watched him nuzzle the door with his snout. Somehow, he was able to wedge it open just enough to slip inside. I let out a yelp of astonishment and crept up the porch steps to follow after him.

There was no way I could let him go in alone.

I slipped past Eli and stepped into Drew's living room. The strong scent of beer and stale cigarettes permeated the air, souring my stomach. The further into the house I stepped, the more potent the stench became. It coated the back of my throat, making me want to gag. The door softly closed behind me and I glanced over my shoulder. We were both inside, which meant we were one step closer to rescuing Violet—and hopefully Glenn—and then getting the hell out of here.

A toilet flushed somewhere in the back of the house. We needed to get it out of sight, but it was hard to do with the layout of the place.

It was what Gran called a shotgun house. Rectangular in shape and built in a way that from the front door you could see through the house straight out the back door. Gran said it was so a person could fire their gun from the front door and it would travel to the back door without hitting a wall.

This made hiding from Drew more difficult.

If he was anything like my father, the chances were steep he'd head to the fridge and grab another beer before moving to the living room. Even from the kitchen, he would be able to see us with the layout of the house. We needed to get out of sight. I slipped out of the living room and into the first room I spotted. Eli followed without hesitation.

The room was small, possibly meant to be a bedroom, but Drew didn't use it as one. Shelves of ammunition lined one wall. A card table sat in the center, a broken-down gun taking up the bulk of it. Along the far wall, there was a gun cabinet large enough to provide weapons for an army.

Drew was a gun collector.

Great.

Eli peaked his head out the door and gazed into the living room. Keeping tabs on where Drew was inside the house was important. When the sound of a fridge opening made its way to my ears, amusement trickled through me. I'd been right in guessing where he would go after leaving the bathroom.

I peeked around Eli, unable to help myself. Curiosity was getting the best of me and I wanted to see if he was reaching for another beer. Drew's back faced me. I couldn't see what he was reaching for, but I could guess. Eli didn't wait around to find out. Instead, he took advantage of the moment and darted from the gun room. He headed through the living room and cut down the hall. I followed close behind without him having to ask.

The fridge shut with a bang and the sound of a can opening echoed through the kitchen the instant we were both hidden in the hall. Loud footfalls passed where we were. They vibrated the floorboards beneath my paws and had my breath hitching in my throat. I prayed Drew wouldn't detour to the hall, but instead would continue to the living room. The last thing we needed was for him to spot us. There was no doubt in my mind he had a gun strapped to his hip. Not with his obvious love of guns.

Stations switching on the TV a few hurried heartbeats later had me relaxing. Eli nudged my side and I glanced at him. He seemed to be ready to move now that we'd skated past the danger zone.

My gaze left him to travel down the length of the hall. Four doors lined it. Two of them were closed and two were open. Eli started for the nearest one. It happened to be one that was open. The sharp scent of urine drifted from the room as we neared it. Apparently, Drew had no aim. At least not when he was hammered, anyway. My snout wrinkled with disgust as we crept past the filthy bathroom.

The next door was closed. Eli tried to nudge it with his snout like he had the screen door, but didn't have any luck. There was no way he'd be able to get it open in this form. Knowing this, he dipped his head and sniffed along the floor trying to pick up either missing pack member's scent. When he shook his head, I knew he hadn't picked up anything. We moved to the next door. It was open, but Eli didn't step inside. Instead, he paused at the threshold and sniffed the air.

Nothing.

We headed to the next door. It was closed. No, it wasn't closed—it was padlocked shut. I didn't have to sniff around to know this was where Violet was being held. The lock said it all.

The problem was: In this form, there was no way we'd be able to get inside that room.

We were screwed.

14

Eli stepped to the end of the hall. He peered around the corner, looking into the living room where Drew was. I imagined he was waiting for the right moment to exit the house and make our way back to his truck. In fact, I was positive of it. Changing into our human form was the only way we would be able to get through that padlocked door. Either we needed to pick the lock or cut it. I hoped Eli had tools in his truck because we were going to need something.

Time ticked away while I listened to the TV show Drew watched along with the lazy sound of him slurping his beer. Just when it seemed as though he was never going to head to the bathroom to relieve his bladder again or to the kitchen for a refill the sound of him snoring met with my ears. Eli must have heard it too, because he stepped forward and began creeping toward the screen door.

Adrenaline spiked through my system as I crept from the hall, following Eli's lead. My gaze drifted to where Drew sat.

His dirty sock-covered feet were lifted in the air by his recliner. They were the first thing I saw. My gaze traveled over his round belly to his face next. His eyes were closed, but his mouth was open. Drool dripped down his stubbly chin, pooling on the dingy white tank top he wore. He was out cold. I only hoped he stayed that way. We needed to make it to Eli's truck, shift back, grab something to bust the lock, and get back to that door unnoticed.

Pretty much we needed a miracle.

When Eli reached the screen door, he pressed his nose against it and continued forward, pushing it open as he went. I squeezed in close behind him, allowing myself to make it through. Without hands to close it softly behind me though, the door slammed shut sounding like a loud crack of thunder. Eli and I bolted down the stairs and into the closest thicket of woods. Neither of us thinking it was a good idea to wait around and see if the loud noise had woken Drew. When he didn't dash to the porch with a shotgun in hand like I'd imagined we started down the driveway, heading back to Eli's truck.

It didn't take us long. Once I made it to the passenger side, I began shifting back. My wolf was reluctant to go. I could feel her unwillingness raging inside of me. Tension rippled through my lean muscles because of it. She was enjoying the sense of freedom she'd gotten from the swift change between moons, but there was also something else. She disagreed with allowing me to take over our current situation and tuck her away. I was forced to give her a solid nudge in order to be able to shift back into my human form. I swung open the passenger door of Eli's truck and quickly pulled on my clothes. An invisible clock ticked above my head, counting down our window of opportunity to retrieve Violet and possibly Glenn.

There was no doubt time was definitely of the essence.

"If the door slamming shut stirred him at all, by the time we get back he should be asleep again," Eli said as he tugged his jeans on. He stood on the opposite side of his truck. "I've got a pair of bolt cutters in the back we should be able to open the lock with. There's a flashlight in the glove compartment, too. Grab it. We might need it."

I pulled Eli's black T-shirt over my head and slipped into my sandals before reaching for the flashlight he'd mentioned. "Got it. Let's get back before he wakes for good or someone else shows up."

"You sure you want to go back?" Eli asked as he pulled his shoes on. "Things are going to get intense from here on out."

I loved how he said this as though nothing about our night had been intense already. Hadn't we been walking around a drunk asshole's house in wolf form trying not to be seen while we searched for missing members of our pack minutes ago?

"I can handle it. I'm down for things to get a little intense." My voice harbored more confidence than I felt. Inside, my heart thundered so hard against my chest it was hard to breathe.

Eli cracked a grin. "Figured you'd say something like that. I've always thought of you as a tough as nails kind of chick."

Tough as nails? I liked that.

"Thanks," I said.

I tucked the flashlight in my back pocket and reached for

the moon ring he'd gotten me. Once I slipped it on, I fastened my silver bracelet on my wrist and glanced at him.

Eli closed the driver side door and moved to search the bed of his truck for the bolt clippers he'd mentioned having. He held them up once he found them and shifted his gaze to lock with mine. "Ready for round two?"

"Absolutely," I said even though I wasn't.

We broke into a jog, both of us knowing there was no time to waste, as we made our way back to Drew's house. Thankfully the road we'd parked Eli's truck on didn't have any traffic. I was sure we looked suspicious—a young couple dressed in black with a pair of bolt cutters running through the dark.

When Drew's house came into view, my adrenaline spiked to an all new high. Eli slowed his pace and I forced myself to do the same. We crept to the front of the house, careful not to make any noise. Eli motioned for me to stay where I was and started up the porch steps. I didn't care for him telling me what to do, but listened to him anyway. If Drew was awake, Eli would need to make a quick escape from the porch and he couldn't do that if I was blocking the steps.

My eyes remained glued to him, watching his every movement with my legs poised to run if need be. Eli rested the bolt cutters against his shoulder like a baseball bat as he peered through the screen door inside the house. Shouldn't I have something to protect myself with too? I reached for the flashlight in my back pocket and wielded it in front of me like a weapon. It was better than nothing.

Eli lifted a hand, motioning for me to step forward. I released the breath I'd been holding and carefully crept up the weathered stairs to where he stood. My heart thundered so loud against my rib cage it was hard to hear anything beyond its frantic rhythm. I sent a silent prayer to the Moon Goddess, hoping she would help us make it through tonight unharmed.

Eli glanced at me and placed his index finger to his lips, giving me the universal *be quiet* signal. I rolled my eyes. What did he think I was going to do? Barge in and make all kinds of noise? No freaking way.

Eli shook his head at my eye roll and eased his way inside. I followed after him, barely breathing.

My gaze darted to the recliner. Drew was still there, snoring. If he had woken earlier, he'd fallen into a deep sleep quickly. I inched along behind Eli, heading to the hallway. Once we are out of plain sight I paused, letting myself soak in the feeling of relief buzzing through me.

Creeping around in someone's house in wolf form seemed a hell of a lot safer than in human form.

"I need you to watch him," Eli whispered, his hot breath caressing across my ear. "Let me know if he stirs. This is probably going to be loud and there's nothing I can do about it."

I nodded, praying the racket coming from the TV would muffle most of the noise he was about to make. I licked my lips and shifted to peer into the living room. Drew hadn't moved.

Yet.

The more I looked at the guy, the more I hated him. He was the definition of a slob. Beer tabs littered the floor around him. The ashtray on the dusty end table beside him was over flowing with cigarette butts, and the guy looked as though he hadn't showered in days. Even the way he slept disgusted and irritated me. I couldn't wait to get this over with so we could grab Violet and get the hell out of here.

But what about Drew?

Shouldn't he have to pay for what he'd done? Some sort of justice needed to be dished out. We couldn't let them walk free for what he'd done and what he planned to do in the future.

At least I couldn't.

Eli and I hadn't discussed any act of revenge or retaliation, but we should have. Whatever consequences for Drew's actions needed to come from us. It was our pack he had screwed with.

I thought of Dan, the contact Eli's dad had at the police station. We could go to him and make sure justice was served after we got Violet to safety. Then again maybe involving the police wasn't a smart move. There was too much we wouldn't be able to explain. Like why Drew had kidnaped Violet in the first place. Although, we could say he was a sicko. Lord knows the world is full of them. It was believable. What would happen to him then, though? Would he go to jail? Was that enough of a punishment for what he'd done and what he planned to do?

The clanking of metal against metal sounded from behind me. Eli had positioned the bolt cutters into place, ready to break the lock. My heart slammed against my rib cage as I shifted back to stare at Drew, watching for any sign he was stirring.

"Ready?" Eli whispered.

Ready for what? Only one of us had an actual weapon that would do any damage. What would I do if Drew jumped up at the first sound of the lock being broken? Shine a damn flashlight in his eyes?

"Yeah," I nodded and positioned myself in a fighting stance. I would just have to work with what I had. There wasn't any other option.

Eli released a long exhale behind me. I did the same, my eyes never wavering from Drew. The tips of my fingers throbbed as I gripped the flashlight tight. Every muscle in my body grew tense as the seconds dragged on.

A loud clank blasted through the hall from behind me. I flinched and then froze, watching as Drew wiggled around in his recliner. His eyes fluttered, but never committed to staying open. When his head lulled to the side and a loud snore rumbled from somewhere deep in the back of his throat I realized luck was definitely on our side.

Eli's eyes were on me. I could feel the heat of them boring into me. I gave him a thumbs up without looking away from Drew, just in case. Another noise echoed through the hall stemming from behind me again. It was softer this time. I imagined it was Eli removing the lock from the door, but didn't risk taking my eyes off Drew for a second. In movies, that was when the bad guy charged. The instant someone let their guard down was when things went all to hell.

I wasn't about to make that mistake.

"Let's go," Eli whispered when he had the door open. "Hand me that light."

I counted to three before leaving my post, making sure Drew was going to remain asleep then started toward Eli. I passed him the flashlight with shaky hands. If Eli noticed, he was smart enough not to comment on it. Everything about me shook, including my insides.

"Come on, let's see if Violet is down here," Eli whispered as he motioned for me to follow him down a set of creaky steps.

A musky scent hit my nose as I stood at the top, looking down. This was definitely a damp basement. I hated basements, but I hated the thought of Violet being down here all alone even more. She had to be scared out of her mind.

I followed Eli on wobbly legs. With the little bit of light offered by the flashlight and my own vision, I was able to make out dingy white walls and a set of old wooden steps. Holes, scratches, and scuff marks chopped up the walls smooth surface. The sight of it had images of someone fighting not to enter Hell surfacing in my mind. Whoever it was, they'd left more than a few marks behind.

Could it have been Violet? What about Glenn?

If it was either of them, it looked as though they'd given Drew a run for his money. I hoped he hadn't beat them for fighting him.

I would kill him if he had touched Violet.

A mismatched washer and dryer came into view as I neared the bottom of the stairs. It was as banged up as a rest of the house, which seemed fitting. Dirty clothes littered the floor around it, contributing to the musky stench of the space. Wooden shelves reaching from floor to ceiling stood on either side of the washer and dryer. Various tools, boxes, random coffee canisters, and loads of mason jars lined them. Eli positioned the flashlight on the top shelf, illuminating a row of mason jars with clear liquid inside.

"Either he makes his own moonshine or buys it in bulk," Eli grinned.

"If he has all this down here why does he waste money buying cheap beer?" My nose wrinkled.

"Good point," Eli said. "I'd be drinking this every night instead."

"The words of a budding alcoholic," I scoffed.

"Say what you want, but you know you'd be right there beside me."

Maybe. If it was apple pie moonshine. That stuff wasn't half bad.

Eli swung around, casting the flashlight around the rest of the basement. Wooden tables and more tools occupied the majority of the space. A broken rocking chair and a stack of cardboard boxes that in the corner. When Eli and I crossed to the opposite side of the basement I couldn't believe what we found there.

Three wrought iron cages lined the far wall.

My eyes fixated on them. The bars of each were thicker than my arm and stood high enough to brush the ceiling. All seemed unoccupied...except for the one in the middle.

Violet sat inside.

15

Violet's small frame was crammed into the back corner of the cage as though she was trying to put distance between her body and the door. Anger bit at my insides as I realized she was naked.

The jerk hadn't given her any clothes when she shifted back.

My gaze trailed over her, searching for any signs he might have hurt her. One of her legs was tucked underneath her chin while the other lay fully extended in front of her. Bruises and scratches marred her skin, but it was the sight of her ankle on the extended leg that had a gasp forcing its way past my lips. It was bloody, swollen, and mangled looking. Had she broken her ankle while trying to fight off Drew? Or did he break it while attempting to get her in her cage?

It didn't matter how it happened. All that mattered was that she wouldn't be able to walk out of here on her own.

"Violet," I whispered. Her eyes were closed. I prayed she

was sleeping as I started toward her. "Violet, it's Mina." Still, she didn't budge.

"This is some cage," Eli whispered. He trailed the flashlight along the height of it. "It's built solid."

"Do you think we'll be able to get her out?" There wasn't a padlock to bust open this time. We would need a key. Panic started to set in. "We have to get her out, Eli. Look at her ankle."

"I know," Eli muttered, but his focus was still on the cage. "It's not made out of silver. He used iron instead. Drew knows more about us than he should."

Eli shifted his attention to the two empty cages on either side of Violet's. From the looks of them, it was clear they hadn't always been empty. Dried blood crusted the cement floor and claw marks scarred it. Each cage housed the same items—a bucket in the back corner and a ratty blanket on the floor. My gaze drifted back to Violet's cage. Sure enough, there was a bucket in the corner and a ratty blanket beneath her.

Had Glenn been held here too? Was the blood in the cage to the left of Violet's his? If so, where was he now? And how many others had come through here?

Maybe Violet would know something.

"Violet!" I whispered, louder this time. She needed to wake up. I needed to know she was able to, that she was okay. "It's Mina and Eli. We're here to take you home."

I tried the door, hoping we'd get lucky and it would be unlocked as Eli continued to stare the craftsmanship of each cage. It didn't budge.

"We need to find something to pick the lock with. My bolt cutters aren't going to do us any good. The bars on the cage are too thick to cut." Eli flashed light around the room, searching for something that might work.

When he backtracked to the shelf near the washer and dryer, I followed.

"Tell me what I should be looking for," I said as I bent at the waist to scour the bottom shelf first.

"Anything metal and sharp."

Nothing stood out. There were a couple of rusted hammers, some stacks of old newspapers covered in mildew, a coffee container filled with rusty nails, and another filled with electrical wire nuts.

"All I've found is some rusty nails," I said as I held up the container. "Think you can pick the lock with one?"

"Maybe," Eli insisted. He took the container from me. "Might work better than the Phillips screwdriver I found."

"We need a small flathead," I said as I adjusted his arm with the light so I could see more of the shelving unit.

"You know what a Phillips screwdriver is?"

"Umm...my dad is a mechanic, remember?" I scoffed.

"Doesn't mean you have to know the difference between a Phillips and a flathead."

"I'm not a complete idiot," I insisted as I rifled through a cardboard box.

"I never said you were, I'm just surprised is all," Eli said as he set the coffee can of nails on the dryer and started rifling through it for the biggest nail. "You surprise me sometimes."

"You surprise me sometimes too," I said without looking at him as I opened the final cardboard box. It was filled with old, rotting paint brushes someone hadn't let dry properly before putting away.

I stepped back from the shelves and placed my hands on

my hips. My body temperature rose as my pulse quickened. There had to be at least one flathead screwdriver lying around. They were a dime a dozen in everyone's house. It was a standard.

A brown bag near the top shelf caught my eye. A wide grin spread onto my face because it looked an awful lot like a tool bag. I stood on the tips of my toes, but still wasn't able to reach it. I reached for the ladder propped against the wall and positioned it where I needed it. It squeaked loudly when I extended it fully and I cringed, hoping the noise hadn't echoed through the basement and caught Drew's attention.

"What are you doing?" Eli asked as I moved the ladder closer to the shelving unit. "We need to be quiet still."

"I know, I wasn't trying to make noise. There's something up there, though. It looks like a tool bag. Maybe there's a small flathead screwdriver we could use inside," I said as I started up the ladder. "Do you know how to pick a lock?"

"Of course," Eli muttered, but there didn't seem to be much confidence behind his words.

My stomach rolled. This was going to take way longer than I would like.

When I reached the top of the ladder I realized it wasn't tall enough for me to reach the tool bag without standing on the very top rung. Since I didn't feel comfortable doing so, I remained one rung below and stretched as far as I could. My fingertips brushed the rough, leathery pouch but it was still just out of my reach.

"Get down," Eli insisted. "Let me get it."

I refused to listen. Instead, I held my breath as I stretched myself as far as I could, standing on the very tips of my toes. I pinched the bag and was able to pull it to the edge of the shelf. Something inside of it shifted, oddly distributing its weight and causing it to slip off the shelf. With reflexes I hadn't known I harbored, I caught it before it hit the floor and climbed down. Once both of my feet were on the ground, I peeked inside.

"What's in it?" Eli asked.

My lips curved into a shit eating grin. "Ta da," I said as I pulled a tiny flathead screwdriver out. "I knew there had to be one somewhere in all this junk."

"All right, let's see if we can get her door open now." Eli took the screwdriver and handed me the flashlight back. "Shine the light steady on the lock for me."

I followed him to Violet's cage and adjusted the light so he could work without shadows. My gaze drifted to Violet. She hadn't moved since we found her. I hoped there wasn't anything wrong with her, like a head injury. Her ankle would keep her from shifting into wolf form, but there was something else keeping her from waking.

Had Drew drugged her?

Goose bumps prickled across my skin. What would be the purpose of drugging her? To keep her quiet? Placid? Was he really that afraid of what she was? If so, maybe we could use that to our advantage...maybe we could scare the shit out of him so he left our pack alone.

As Eli worked on picking the lock to Violet's cage, I tried to think of how we could go about scaring Drew. What if scaring him wasn't enough, though? He had done horrible things and he needed to pay for them. We could beat him up before we left. We could kill him. Turn him over to the police for kidnapping Violet. Burn his house down with him still passed out in the recliner.

Darker and darker thoughts took up residency in my mind, but nothing seemed as though it would be enough.

The only thing I could decide on was the fact that I wasn't walking away from this house without retaliating against Drew for what he had done. He and his brothers needed to know they couldn't get away with what they were doing any longer. They needed to know there were consequences. Ones I was willing to dish out.

A click echoed through the basement, pulling me from my thoughts.

Eli had done it. He'd picked the lock on Violet's cage.

"Got it," he grinned at me from over his shoulder. "Let's get Violet and get the hell out of here."

Eli swung the cage door open. I expected Violet to stir from the noise, but she didn't. There was something wrong with her. Was she dead? My heart pounded in my throat as Eli grew closer to her. I propped a discarded bucket against the cage door to keep it open before stepping inside, not wanting to take any chances it might swing shut and trap us.

"Violet," Eli said as he crouched down beside her. His voice was soft and soothing, but it still didn't do anything to stir her awake. "Hey, we're here to take you home." He touched her shoulder, but she still remained unresponsive.

"Is she alive?" I asked in a small voice.

Eli moved his fingers to take her pulse along the side of her neck. "Yeah."

Thank God.

"Do you think Drew drugged her then?"

"Yeah, I think the bastard did."

"Do you think he did anything else to her?" My eyes raked over her naked body, taking in her multiple bruises and cuts as my teeth ground together. I couldn't even think about it.

"I hope not, but I don't think we'll know for sure until she wakes."

My free hand clenched into a fist at my side. "He needs to pay for what he did. Are we going to do anything to him before we leave?" I had to know what Eli was thinking.

"Oh yeah," he insisted. He smoothed Violet's damp hair away from her face. "I haven't decided what yet, though."

"Me either."

"Violet, hey," Eli said softly, trying to rouse her again. She didn't budge. "Come on, wake up. It's time to go. We need to get out of here." He tapped her cheek repeatedly. She groaned, but never opened her eyes.

Maybe she couldn't. Maybe whatever Drew had given her wouldn't let her, no matter how hard she tried. It sucked because while I had counted on having to help her walk out of here, I hadn't thought Eli would have to carry her. What if Drew spotted us and tried to stop us?

I guess I'd have to go toe to toe with him.

"Come on. You can do it. Wake up," Eli insisted as a rubbed her shoulder. She groaned again and this time attempted to lift her arm. I wasn't sure if she was trying to wake up or push him away thinking he was Drew. Either way, she didn't manage much of anything. Her rubbery arm fell to her lap and remained motionless as she drifted back to sleep. "She's not going wake up. I'll have to carry her."

"Okay, you focus on getting her up and out of the cage carefully and I'll see if I can find a weapon to use in case we need it."

I exited the cage. There had to be something I could use

lying around. A broom. A shovel. Something other than a dang flashlight or a pair of bolt cutters. I walked around the outer edge of the basement, searching. An axe wedged between the dryer and the shelf near where I'd left the ladder caught my eye. Now we were talking. Finally, something I could do some damage with.

I stepped around the ladder and bent to retrieve the axe from beside the dryer. Rough wood that felt slightly spongy met with my hand. The thing must've been waterlogged at one point.

I pulled it out, gripping it tightly. It still felt sturdy enough to be of use. I positioned the flashlight on it. The ax itself didn't seem very sharp and it was rusted all to hell, but those were the least of my worries. It could still do some serious damage if I needed it to. There were few who could survive blunt force to the head by something like this. Adrenaline pumped through me as I rushed to show Eli my find. In my hurry, my foot caught on the ladder I'd left out from before, causing it to shift on the concrete and make a god-awful noise. I reached out to steady it before it could topple over. It wobbled, hitting the shelving unit behind me and knocked a box from one of the shelves, which fell to the floor with a thud. Curse words flew from my mouth. I froze and squeezed my eyes shut, praying Drew hadn't heard the ruckus upstairs.

"You okay?" Eli asked instead of reprimanding me for making so much noise.

"Yeah, I'm fine." My heart was about to explode, but I was okay.

"Bring me the light, I need..."

If Eli had finished his sentence I wasn't able to hear him.

All I could hear was the sound of someone stomping around upstairs.

Either someone had come to visit Drew or the noise I caused woke him. Neither situation was a good one to be in.

I held my breath, listening as whoever it was continued through the house. When they stopped at the top of the basement stairs, anxiety prickled across my skin and my heartbeat hummed in my ears.

"What the fuck?" Drew's groggy voice floated down the stairs. He'd spotted the cut padlock on the door.

Eli scanned the basement. I knew he was searching for an alternate way out. There wasn't one. The basement was underground, which meant there was only one way out—the same way we'd entered.

We'd have to face off with Drew.

16

The basement door swung open, allowing light from the upstairs hallway to spill down the steps. I rushed to Eli's side, not knowing what else to do. We were screwed. I could only imagine the amount of money Drew would get when he presented not one young female werewolf but two along with a young male to his boss.

"I need you to take Violet and get out of here," Eli whispered. He secured the blanket he'd wrapped around Violet tighter and motioned for me to take her from him. His gaze flicked to the stairs and even in the darkness I could make out the heavy sense of determination rippling through the bright green of his eyes. "No matter what, that's all you're supposed to do. Got it?"

"What? No," I insisted. "We're in this together, Eli. Whatever you're planning to do you need to count me in."

"I can't. Violet needs to get out of here, and so do you," he insisted in a harsh whisper seconds before the sound of a gun cocking echoed through the basement. "I mean it, Mina. Get yourself and Violet out of here."

I shook my head. There was no way I would leave him. Not with Drew and his gun. "Eli..."

"Promise me."

I couldn't. He was asking me to leave him behind. There was no way I could do that. Eli would never leave me behind.

"Mina, promise me," Eli insisted again. Drew was nearly halfway down the stairs. His heavy footfalls echoed through the basement, becoming an intense soundtrack to the conversation Eli and I were having. My mouth went dry. "Damn it, promise me!" He gripped my shoulders tight.

"I...I promise," I muttered, hating myself the second the words pushed past my lips.

Eli's mouth crushed against mine. He pulled me as close to him as he possibly could and worked his mouth across mine. The slight brush of his tongue touched my closed lips, but the instant I realized what was happening he pulled away. He grabbed the ax from my hands, and started toward the stairs.

I didn't waste time staring after him. Instead, I dove into action. I knew if I could get Violet out of the house and to a safe location I'd be able to come back and help him with Drew.

While my plan might not be Eli approved, I didn't give a damn.

Violet was starting to come to. She wasn't fully awake, but her eyes fluttered and she was moaning. Whatever she'd been given was either wearing off or she was one hell of a fighter.

I lifted one of her arms and wedged my shoulder beneath

it. She was nearly as tall as me and we weighed about the same size, so carrying her was out of the question. She needed to wake up. I pressed my feet firmly into the ground and lifted her, helping to get her to her feet. All the times I dragged my drunk dad from one place to another had come in handy.

Mumbles and murmurs left her lips, but I couldn't make out what she was saying. Instead of trying to decipher her words I chose to ignore her. I shifted her to lean on me so she wouldn't put weight on her ankle. I had no idea how I was going to get her up the stairs. Then again, I didn't know how we would get past Drew either.

That, I was leaving up to Eli.

A loud grunt captured my attention followed by banging. Drew was tumbling down the stairs. My gaze shifted to where Eli stood. From where he was, it looked as though he tripped Drew with the handle of the rusty ax he'd taken from me. I glanced back at Drew. He didn't seem to be moving. Was he knocked out from the fall?

I continued dragging Violet toward the stairs, hoping we'd make it up them without falling like Drew. Also, it would be nice to do it before he came to. My stomach knotted as I cast a quick glance at him.

He seemed to already be stirring. I could hardly breathe.

I bit back a scream when he forced himself into a sitting position. He rubbed his head and groaned. I froze, watching to see what he would do next. Would he shoot us? Wait. Where was the gun he had?

"What the hell?" Drew grumbled once he spotted me and Violet. "That's my paycheck you're taken away, little girl. Where do you think you're goin' with her?"

I flinched at his horrible words. Rage burned within me from how he viewed Violet. A paycheck? What an asshole. I opened my mouth to say so, but Violet moaned. Was she in pain? How could she not be? Her ankle had to hurt like a mother. A noise I couldn't distinguish captured my attention. A gun went sliding across the floor.

Eli had kicked Drew's gun out of his reach.

Thank goodness.

"Go! Get out of here," Eli insisted. He stepped between Drew and the stairs, blocking his path to us and creating a safe exit to squeeze through.

I took it, knowing I needed to get Violet up those stairs and out of this house so I could come back and make sure Eli was okay. Adrenaline spiked through my system, causing my limbs to tingle.

It took everything I had to get Violet up the stairs, but somehow I managed. She helped as best she could, but she was still out of it. Her head kept lulling to the side. It was a wonder she could support herself at all.

Once we made it to the hall, I paused and listened to the house, searching for anyone who might've entered while we were focused on Drew downstairs. When no one else seemed to be inside, I started forward. Noises from the basement made their way to my ears, but I tuned them out. There was nothing I could do to help Eli until I got Violet to safety first. Besides, Eli was more than capable of handling Drew himself. Right?

"Come on, we need to hurry," I insisted as I adjusted Violet's weight on my shoulder. Pain sliced through my shoulder blade but I ignored it.

We were down the hall, through the living room, and out

the screen door faster than I thought possible. Fear Eli might be hurt—or killed—was a powerful motivator. It had me almost dragging Violet along.

Once we were outside, I deposited her at the edge of the woods, hidden behind a ticket. My hands went to my hips as I buckled over, struggling to catch my breath. Thoughts raced through my mind. What was my next move? Run straight to the basement and see what I could do to help get Eli out alive? Violet moaned, drawing my attention back to her. Her eyes stayed closed. Relief trickled through me, because there was no way I had time to explain what happened to her or what I was doing here.

I needed to get back to Eli.

A manly growl spurred from the basement of the house. It floated along the humid night air straight to my ears, making the fine hairs on the back of my neck stand on end. It wasn't Eli. It was Drew. And from the sounds of it, he seemed victorious about something.

Shit!

My feet were moving before I could form a plan of action. I darted up the steps to the porch and bolted through the screen door. The bedroom filled with guns was the only thing on my mind. I opened the cabinet nearest me and reached in for one. The shotgun was heavier than I thought it would be, but at least I had a decent weapon. I popped the chamber open the way I'd seen done on TV and spotted two large bullets crammed inside. A long breath exhaled from my lungs as another loud noise rolled through the house, stemming from the basement.

Drew and Eli had gone to war.

I launched myself out of the room, cut through the living

room, and dashed down the hall. Once I reached the top of the basement steps, I paused to take in the sounds drifting up from below. The fight was still taking place, but it was hard to tell who was winning from listening.

I descended the stairs, gripping the shotgun tight, knowing I'd use it if it meant saving Eli's life or my own.

When Eli and Drew came into view I aimed the gun at them, but knew with as much as they were rolling around I'd never get a clear shot. I wasn't a great shot to begin with. In fact, this was only my second time holding a gun in my life.

Drew mounted Eli and wrapped his meaty hands around his throat. Gargles and gasps for breath passed from Eli's lips. I had to do something. Being frozen in the background wasn't doing Eli any good. Now that Violet was safe, he was my top priority.

I jogged down the remaining stairs and smashed the butt of the shotgun into the back of Drew's head. He tumbled forward, landing on Eli.

"What the hell are you doing back here?" Eli choked out as he struggled to get Drew off him and to catch his breath. "You shouldn't have come back. I told you to get Violet out of the house and yourself."

"I did get Violet out," I insisted. "And, I believe a thank you is in store. I just saved your ass," I said with more attitude than I felt. My insides were still quivering as the sight of Eli being choked to death flashed through my mind on repeat.

He could have died.

Eli slipped out from under Drew and forced himself into a standing position. "Thank you, I guess," he muttered as he rubbed his throat while tossing a pissed off glare Drew's way.

I scanned the length of Eli, making sure he was truly

okay. Blood trickled from above his right eye. His lip was busted and there were a few bruises forming across the left side of his face. When he brought his hand up to wipe away the blood from his eye, I noticed his knuckles were bloodied too.

It must have been one hell of a fight.

"Are you okay?" I asked all attitude and teasing aside. I erased the small distance between us and reached out to touch the cut above his eye. He didn't shrink away from my touch, but instead seemed to melt toward it. "That cut is pretty deep."

For a human, it was probably deep enough to warrant stitches, but because Eli wasn't human I doubted he'd need any. In a day or two it would heal on its own thanks to being Moon Kissed and the healing abilities that came along with it. It would still need to be cleaned out, though. Werewolves might be able to heal cuts and broken bones, to a certain extent, but that didn't mean infections couldn't set in and cause severe damage.

"We really should clean that up. Do you have a first aid kit in your truck?" I asked. Eli didn't answer. My gaze drifted from his cut to his eyes. He was staring at my lips. I licked them nervously. The air around us crackled with pent-up energy and I knew he was going to kiss me again. This time I would be ready. This time I'd move my lips beneath his and respond the way I was supposed to, the way I wanted each time he surprised me with a kiss.

Movement behind him captured my attention. My eyes shifted from Eli to Drew a heartbeat before Eli pressed his lips against mine. I couldn't respond the way I wanted to. Not with Drew getting to his feet behind Eli. Drew lifted a tightly closed fist, ready to smash it into the back of Eli's head. My eyes widened and I shoved Eli out of the way. He stumbled to my left as Drew's fist connected with my nose. Blood sprayed from it on contact, saturating Eli's black shirt with its sticky wetness. The edges of my vision speckled with darkness and blurred all at once. I stumbled backward, my hands cupping my nose as tears pricked the corners of my eyes. The coppery taste of blood trickled down the back of my throat and filled my mouth.

"What did you do with my paycheck? Did you set her free?" Drew grumbled. His words were still slurred together, but I couldn't be sure whether it was from the alcohol in his system or the concussion he most likely had from the blow I'd given him to the back of the head with the shotgun. "I'll take you in her place if you did, little bitch." He grabbed my arm and jerked me toward him.

I dug my feet into the ground and jerked wildly to get free from his grasp but it did me no good.

Drew was ten times my size.

"Hey you," Eli shouted. He'd snuck up behind Drew. When Drew glanced at him from over his shoulder, Eli gripped the sides of his head and twisted. The sound of bone crunching against bone echoed through the basement as his neck snapped. My mouth fell open. Drew's grip on my arm loosened and he crumpled to the floor in a heap.

I blinked. Nothing in front of me changed. Drew still remained motionless at my feet, his head twisted at an odd angle.

"You killed him," I whispered unable to take my eyes off Drew. "You snapped his neck."

Killing Drew had crossed my mind, but I didn't think it

was something I'd go through with unless the situation called for it. Had this situation called for it?

"I had to. He was going to take you. He'd already taken Violet. He played a big hand in Glenn's disappearance. Who knows what all he's done or what he had planned to do in the future," Eli insisted. I wasn't sure if he was trying to convince me what he'd done was justified or if he was attempting to convince himself. "You would've done the same thing if he'd been coming after me. It had to be done, Mina."

I swallowed hard. "I know."

I'd brought a shotgun downstairs with me for that very reason. I knew Drew had to be stopped at any cost. Even so, the sight of him dead shook me up. It shouldn't. He'd called Violet a paycheck and had intended to sell me in her place once.

Why was I so worked up over this then?

Maybe it wasn't that Drew was lying at my feet dead, but that I'd seen him killed. Right in front of me.

"What do we do now?" I asked in a shaky voice. I needed to pull myself together to somehow make it through this moment and the next.

My gaze drifted around the basement, opting to look anywhere besides at Drew.

Warmth tickled across my upper lip, making me remember my bloody nose. I wiped at it with the back of my hand. Deep red streaked across my skin. I pinched the bridge of my nose and tipped my head back to stop the flow.

"We need to clean this place up. Get rid of any evidence that might point to us being here."

Okay, that sounded like a good idea. It didn't answer the question pressing against me from all sides, though.

"What do we do with him?" I kicked my foot toward Drew but couldn't look at him.

"We need to get him to the bottom of those stairs and make it look like he fell," Eli insisted. I released my nose and sniffled. The bleeding seemed to have stopped. "He was a heavy drinker, if we can stage the scene right anyone would believe he'd been drinking and tripped coming down the stairs. People fall down stairs all the time, especially when they've been drinking heavily. Hell, people even die from internal bleeding after falling down the stairs. It's as good a cover story as any. We have to make it look legit, though. We don't need anyone coming after us in connection with his death later on down the road."

I sniffled again and fought the urge to wipe my nose, knowing it would only cause it to start bleeding all over again. "Okay. What do you want me to do?"

Directions. Instructions. Being told what to do and how. It was the only thing that was going to get me through this mess.

"Let's get him to the bottom of the stairs," Eli said. He bent at the waist and grabbed Drew by his arms.

My hands shook as I reached for his feet. A heavy sensation settled in the pit of my stomach. I couldn't believe I was helping to move a dead body. This was not how I'd thought the night would go.

"What else?" I asked once Drew was laid at the bottom of the steps. I licked my lips and swallowed the saliva pooling in my mouth. Nausea pulsed through me. Along with a strong desire to shower and then curl into the fetal position.

"We need to clean up any blood. Even Violet's in the cage. We don't want to leave anything behind that could be traced back to the pack." Eli's voice was calm and steady as though he'd given out orders like this a million times. While it sort of unnerved me because I was on the verge of having a breakdown and he wasn't, it also had me realizing he was going to be one hell of a pack leader when the time came.

"Okay," I searched for cleaner and a rag.

"Check near the washer for some bleach. It's the only thing that'll kill the blood and make it as close to untraceable as it can be to the naked eye."

"How do you know this?" I asked as I reached for the gallon jug of bleach beside the washer.

"Trust me, you don't want to now."

I inhaled a sharp breath as I scratched out a mental note to never piss off Eli.

With the jug of bleach in hand and one of Drew's crusty T-shirts from a pile near the washer, I scrubbed the floor where he'd smashed in my nose. Eli brought a rag over and poured some bleach on it before moving to clean the area where he and Drew had fought. We moved to the cage Violet had been held in next. Afterward, we cleaned the other two cages. The cage to the left of Violet's was horrible.

"God, this one is a mess," I said as I paused to glance around the cage. "Looks like it was used to store an animal, not a human."

"Ummm...that's because it was," Eli insisted.

My stomach somersaulted as my chest tightened. He was right.

Once the basement was clean, the only thing I could smell was bleach. I hoped the sharp scent wouldn't linger around too long. It might seem suspicious if it did. Drew didn't seem like the type to go on a cleaning binge. Ever.

"The last thing we need to do is change the padlock on the basement door and put the gun you brought down back upstairs after we wipe it off," Eli insisted as he ran his rag along the ladder I'd set out. He slipped it back between the shelving unit and the dryer and then reached for a cardboard box. "Here's a new lock."

He handed me a new padlock. I didn't ask how he'd known it was there, figuring he'd found it while searching for something to pick the lock to Violet's cage with earlier.

Violet. I hoped she was still where I'd left her. Anxiety and shock had managed to freeze time, making it hard for me to gauge how long ago it was I'd left her.

Eli picked up the shotgun and wiped it off. The movement pulled me out of my thoughts.

"What about his gun?" I nodded to the gun kicked into the corner.

Eli glanced at it but didn't move to pick it up. "I think it's fine where it's at. Makes the scene look more authentic. It could have slid out of his holster when he fell."

I nodded, but didn't say anything. My skin was starting to crawl. I was ready to get the hell out of here.

"Where did you leave Violet?"

"At the edge of the woods," I said. "I hope she's still there."

"With the way her ankle was and how doped up she seemed to be, I highly doubt she went anywhere. We need to take her to your gran. I'm sure Violet's ankle will have to be broken again so it can be set right."

A chill ran up my spine at the thought as I started toward the stairs with my bleach rag in hand. "Yeah. All right, let's switch out this lock and get the heck out of here. I don't want to be here any longer than we have to be."

"Agreed," Eli said as he followed up the steps behind me. "Wait a minute,"

"What?" I paused and glanced over my shoulder at him. He was heading back down the stairs.

"Forgot something."

I watched him as he went to the dryer and climbed on top. He reached toward one of the shelves lined with mason jars of moonshine and grabbed a jar. Eli tucked it underneath his arm and then grabbed another before hopping down and jogging back up the stairs to where I was.

"Didn't want to leave without one of these...or two," he winked.

I rolled my eyes and then continued up the stairs.

Him and his damn moonshine.

Once we switched out the busted padlock for a new one, we returned the shotgun I'd taken to its cabinet and made our way outside. Fresh air had never felt better.

I led Eli to where I'd left Violet. She was still lying on the ground at the edge of the woods, folded in on herself. I couldn't get over how fragile and young she looked. There were three years between us, but from the way she looked right now, it could have easily appeared to be ten.

Eli shined the flashlight on her ankle. It looked worse. The swelling had intensified. I attributed it to having her walk on it so I could get her out of the house. Guilt swam through me. She'd probably damaged it more because I made her walk on it. I hadn't had a choice, though.

I sent a prayer to the Moon Goddess asking that Gran be able to fix Violet's ankle. If not there was a good chance she might be like my father—forever a wolf inside, but never able to shift.

If that ended up being the case, Drew deserved what he'd got.

"Here, you carry this and I'll carry her," Eli insisted as he held out the two jars of moonshine, the flashlight, and his bleach rag. I took everything he held out and watched as he bent to lift Violet up as though she weighed nothing. He cradled her against his chest and started down the driveway. "Let's go."

"Right behind you." I started walking. My grip on all I was carrying intensified as I reflected on everything that had happened in the span of a few hours. When my mind drifted to Drew, I tried to think of how we'd rescued Violet instead. How Eli and I were a good team.

Were we a team, or were we slowly starting to become something more? Could I allow that to happen? Did I even have a choice at this point? And where did that leave things between me and Alec?

"How's your nose?" Eli asked, pulling me from my thoughts. as he shifted Violet in his arms. "That asshole really popped you good."

Instinctively, my fingers lifted to press against my nose. It was tender and I was positive it was swollen, probably even broken, but I was okay. "Sore, but I don't think it isn't anything a little moonshine won't help," I said trying to lighten the mood. For me, at least. I needed this night to be over with.

"Damn right," Eli chuckled. Violet moaned in his arms. "Shh. You're okay. You're safe. I've got you."

Jealousy slipped through me at the sound of his soft

words to her. That blow to the nose must've really done a number on me.

Once we reached Eli's truck, he laid Violet down on the passenger seat.

"Sorry, but you're going to have to go in through the driver side door and scoot across to sit in the middle," Eli insisted as he closed the door. "I don't want to lay her in the back."

"That's fine," I said.

I climbed in the driver's side and scooted across the bench seat to sit in the middle. My fingers smoothed through Violet's damp hair. Her eyelids fluttered, but she didn't wake fully. I wished whatever Drew had given her would wear off.

Eli climbed behind the steering wheel and cranked the engine of his truck. He flicked on his headlights and shifted into reverse. Seconds later, we were cruising down Wilmont Avenue, heading home, and I finally felt like I could breathe again.

17

Eli cut into the trailer park faster than he should. Gravel spun out from beneath his tires, shooting in all directions. He slammed on the brakes when he reached my place and we both hopped out of the truck. He moved to retrieve Violet while I went inside to get Gran. There was a light on in the living room which gave me hope she might still be awake.

When I stepped inside our trailer I spotted her in the recliner, reading one of her romance novels while sipping tea. Her mouth flew open when she glanced up from her book at me.

"Oh my, what happened?" she insisted as she tossed her book aside and leaped from her chair.

"I'll explain everything later. If I can," I insisted knowing I might not be able to give her any details. Pack law was pack law. Anything I said had to be given on a need to know basis only. I grabbed hold of her arm and pulled her toward the kitchen where she stored her herbal remedies. "We found Violet, but she's hurt."

The sound of Eli coming up the steps floated to my ears. I rushed to the door and held it open for him.

"How did you find her?" I heard Gran ask. "How bad is she hurt? What happened?"

"Where should I set her?" he asked once he'd stepped inside.

"On the couch," I said ignoring Gran's questions. My answers would have to be carefully thought out. I didn't want to get into any trouble with the Alpha. I also didn't want Eli to get into trouble either.

"What happened?" Gran asked again. "I'll need to know some specifics so I know what to use to heal her."

"She's bruised up. There are a few scrapes and I think she might've been drugged. Her ankle seems to be the worst of it, though." I stepped to where Gran was and held out my arms, ready for her to fill them with any herbs and concoctions she could use to heal Violet. "It looks like it's been broken and healed the wrong way."

Gran passed me jars of flowers and herbs before bending at the waist to retrieve a ceramic bowl from a cabinet beneath the sink. I watched as she filled it with water, then motioned for me to make my way to the couch along with her.

"All right. I need to set that ankle right. Which means I'll need to re-break it," Gran insisted. She placed the ceramic bowl of water on the coffee table. I did the same with the herbs she'd passed me to hold. "Eli, I want you to go to the hall closet and grab a sheet. The poor girl is freezing. Mina, grab a few elderflowers and some yarrow flowers and put them in the bowl of water for me while I better access her ankle."

I did as I was told, so did Eli. When he came back with a sheet, I'd already made a poultice of the flowers like Gran had asked. The consistency was perfect.

Maybe I knew more about all this natural healing crap than I thought.

"Oh, the poor dear. This looks awful. What happened to her? Do you know who did this?"

My eyes shifted to Eli, unsure if I was allowed to say anything. This had been pack business after all.

"Violet was abducted. We know who it was and you can rest assured they've been dealt with," Eli said sounding more professional than I'd ever heard him before.

"Okay," Gran said plainly. Her gaze had drifted to me, but I couldn't meet her stare. "And, the two of you were working together on this?"

"Yeah. We were," Eli answered again.

When Gran didn't say anything this time, I risked a glance at her. A small smirk had spread across her face. Why was she smiling? Was she happy to hear Eli and I been working together or was it because we'd obviously been spending time together?

Violet squirmed and released a moan. Gran's touch must have hurt her.

"Mina, is that poultice ready?" Gran asked.

"I think so," I said even though I never could tell with these things.

"I'm going to need the two of you to hold Violet down. If she's already starting to come out of her drug-induced haze she's going to feel what I'm about to do and react. I need you to hold her steady so I can make sure to create a clean break. I only want to do this once, the poor child has been through enough," Gran insisted.

I stood and leaned over the bottom portion of Violet's body while Eli pressed against her shoulders, making sure she laid flat on the couch. She wiggled at the feel of pressure on her, but not enough to cause an issue.

"Shhh, it's Mina. You're at my Gran's and you're safe. We need you to hold still. Gran needs to reset your ankle," I said in case she could hear me. I wanted her to understand we were trying to help her.

"Hold her tight," Gran insisted. That was all the warning she gave before she jerked Violet's ankle as hard as she could.

A loud crack echoed through the trailer, causing me to wince. Violet bucked against us and she cried out. Her scream blasted through my ears. I felt horrible for holding her down, but knew it was necessary.

"You can release her now," Gran said while reaching for the ceramic bowl of mush she had me make. "Once I put this on her ankle she should feel instant relief."

I released my grip on Violet and noticed when Eli did the same. His face had contorted with worry for her, and I knew he felt as horrible as I did for having to hurt her any more than she already had been. I shifted my gaze from him to Gran, watching as she pasted Violet's swollen ankle with a thick layer of flowers.

"You two are next. Don't even think about going anywhere." Gran cast a pointed gaze to me and Eli. "I can tell from looking at you, Mina, you've got a broken nose. And Eli, that cut above your eye needs to be cleaned before it gets infected. First thing is first though, I need a hot mug of water, some dandelion root, red clover blossoms, and burdock root to clean this poor girl's blood. Whatever she was given is bogging her down."

I headed to the kitchen, thankful for something to do. It helped keep everything I was feeling at a distance a while longer. If not I might break down in front of everyone.

Once I gathered a mug of hot water and the herbs Gran had requested, I watched as she created a dull amber-colored tea.

"Lift her head. She needs to drink this," Gran insisted.

Eli lifted Violet's head and I watched as Gran coaxed her to drink the tea. Once she was finished, Violet laid against the pillows and snored softly. Gran shifted her attention to me next.

"Follow me," she insisted as she stood.

I followed her to the kitchen where she proceeded to fix my nose. Her touch sent pain radiating through my head, but I knew she wasn't trying to hurt me. She was only assessing the damage.

"It's broken," Gran insisted. Without warning, she reached up and popped it back into place.

White hot pain shot through me as blood trickled down my face onto Eli shirt again. If it hadn't been ruined before, it damn sure would be now. He needed to throw in the trash or burn it. I for one didn't want any reminders of this night lying around.

"There. Now you need a hot shower and a good night's sleep. Both of you," she said as she shifted her attention to Eli. She cleaned the cut above his eye and leaned forward to give him a kiss on the forehead before motioning for me to step closer for one too. "I'm proud of you two. I don't know the whole story, and I'm sure you can't tell me, but I want you to know I'm proud of you for rescuing that little girl. Her parents will be so happy you did. The entire pack will be. You did a good thing tonight, and I thank you."

I didn't say anything because I didn't know what to say. We'd killed a man tonight in our efforts to rescue one of our own. Was that something to be proud of?

"Thanks," Eli said as he ran a hand through his hair. Was he as distraught as I was over the night's events? "I think I'm gonna head home. I'll talk to you later, Mina."

Eli started toward the front door and I wasn't sure if I should go after him. I took too long deciding and he slipped through the door and out of my view.

"Go take a shower, honey. Give yourself some time to decompress. I can sense you've been through a lot tonight." Gran gave me one more kiss on the forehead before gently pushing me toward the hall.

I gave in to what she was suggesting and grabbed my favorite tank top and a pair of jogging shorts before heading to the bathroom. My nose pulsed with my heartbeat as I bent over the bathtub to adjust the water. I was grateful for speedy werewolf healing, knowing tomorrow I'd wake up and my nose would be fine or at least close to it. Pain was not something I could tolerate much of.

I peeled my clothes off and stepped into the shower without glancing at myself in a mirror. There was no way I wanted to see myself. I could feel how awful I looked.

As soon as the warm water hit my shoulders, I relaxed for the first time all night. This slip up caused emotions I'd been fighting to keep at bay to bubble to the surface. They washed over me in massive waves before I could secure my wall back in place. Images of Eli snapping Drew's neck flashed on repeat behind my closed eyes. I knew he'd done it to protect me and the pack, but couldn't help besides feel sick. Killing Drew made us no better than him.

My mind drifted, repeating the horrible sound and the look on his face as I washed.

A knock at the door sounded.

"Mina, honey, are you all right?" Gran's soft voice filtered through the door.

"Yeah, I'm okay," I shouted as I turned the water off.

I was okay. I was safe. I was home.

"Okay. Just checking." Her retreating footsteps sounded and I exhaled a slow breath.

How long had I been in the shower? It didn't seem like it would have been long enough to worry her.

I dried myself off and pulled on my clean clothes. With my hair still dripping, I glanced at myself in the mirror.

Failure glistened behind my eyes.

Not because we'd been forced to kill Drew, but because this wasn't over with yet. We weren't able to rescue Glenn.

We'd saved one pack member, but not the other.

Glenn hadn't been there. How on earth were we going to find him?

Violet. Maybe she would be able to tell us something once she finally came to.

My feet propelled me out of the bathroom and toward the couch where she slept. It would probably be another day or two before she woke and even then, who knew when she'd be ready to talk.

A knock at the front door startled me.

"Could you get that for me, dear?" Gran asked from

where she stood at the kitchen sink, washing the ceramic bowl we'd used earlier.

"Yeah. Sure." My voice was flat. I was numb as I started toward the door. Exhaustion was creeping through my body, but not through my mind. It was still churning.

When I opened the door, the last person I expected to see again so soon stood there.

Eli's hair was wet, dripping down his neck onto the collar of his shirt as he stood on my porch. He'd changed clothes and I could smell his shampoo, or was that his body wash, on him. I loved that smell whatever it was. It had things stirring to life inside of me I didn't think should be considering our night.

"You forgot this in my truck," he said, holding out my cell. "There are a few messages I thought you might want to answer." His eyes dipped to his shoes.

I took my cell from him, but didn't check to see who they were from. Instead, I clutched it in my hand and crossed my arms over my chest, suddenly aware I was standing before him braless. Not that it should matter, he'd seen me naked before, but somehow it did.

"So...are you okay?" Eli asked. There was a weight to his words. I knew why.

"Yeah. I mean, as okay as I can be I guess." I shifted around on my feet. "I don't think I'll be able to sleep for a while, though. I'm still pretty keyed up."

The ghost of a smile quirked at the corners of his lips. "Me either. You're always welcome at my place. I don't think I'll be heading to bed anytime soon."

I glanced over my shoulder. Violet was still passed out on the couch and Gran was in the kitchen.

"You don't need my permission," Gran said as though she could feel my eyes on her.

I licked my lips and shifted back to face Eli. "Let me get some shoes."

"Okay. I'll wait here."

I headed to my room and slipped on a bra and some flip-flops. My phone called out to me. I was curious if it was Gracie or Alec who'd messaged me.

It was Alec.

Movie was great. You would have liked it. Call me tomorrow, maybe we can do something?

I set my phone on top of my dresser. I'd reply back tomorrow. I didn't have it in me tonight to talk to him. There was so much more on my mind than the latest movie playing at the theater.

Smoothing my fingers through my wet hair, I made my way back to the front door. Gran didn't say a word when I left. Eli stood at the hood of my car, waiting when I stepped outside.

"Want to have a fire?" Eli asked as we walked side-by-side to his trailer.

I tucked my wet hair behind my ears and glanced at him. "Where?"

"My place. I found a big burn barrel leaning up against the trailer when I moved in." Eli grinned. "There's some evidence we need to get rid of tonight, don't you think?"

I remembered the dingy shirts of Drew's we'd used to clean up the scene of his death. "Can you burn a rag with bleach on it?"

"It's probably not the healthiest thing to burn, but as long as we aren't huffing the smoke I think we'll be okay."

"I doubt I'll be doing that," I chuckled.

"Me either. I think will be good." He motioned for me to sit in one of the bag chairs he'd bought recently once we reached his place. "Take a seat. I'll drag the barrel around."

I sat and folded my legs beneath me. My gaze drifted to the star speckled sky as I inhaled a deep breath. I couldn't believe how my night had gone. I'd watched the life fade out of Shane's brother's eyes and helped to rescues Violet. God, I'd been so worried about her when I learned she was missing.

"All right," Eli muttered as he dropped the barrel in front of me. "Let me get the rags from inside. I'll be right back."

"I'll be here," I said, tucking my hands beneath my thighs. It was cooler out now that my hair was wet and I was in a tank top and shorts. Part of me thought maybe I should head home for a sweater and the blood-soaked T-shirt Eli had let me borrow earlier tonight, but I was too comfortable to move.

"Want me to grab you a sweater?" Eli asked when he stepped out. "You look cold."

"Yeah, that would be great. I'm a little chilly."

"Sure." Eli tossed the rags in the barrel and started up the stairs again. He came back a few minutes later with a gray hoodie draped over one arm and a jar of moonshine in his hand. I was pretty sure it was one we'd taken from Drew's. "I think we deserve a drink after everything we've been through tonight. I know you might be upset still about what happened, but we made damn sure no one in our pack would be hunted by Drew again. And, we rescued Violet from who knows what horrendous things she might've had to endure once she was sold to whoever Drew's buyer was."

I swallowed hard, ignoring the comment about Drew's

death, and nodded in agreement instead. "Yeah, I think a drink is in order."

Eli handed me his hoodie. I pulled it on, and inhaled the scent of him that lingered in the woven fabrics. There was something about it that calmed me in a way I couldn't explain.

I watched as he struck a match and tossed it into the barrel. The T-shirts went up instantly and relief trickled through my shoulders and chest at the sight of them burning. All traces that could lead to Eli, me, or the pack were now gone.

"There, now we can put tonight behind us," Eli said as he made his way to the chair beside me. He sat, and stretched his long legs out in front of him before opening the moonshine. He held it out to me before taking a sip himself. "Here, have a sip and then tell me what's going on in that pretty little head of yours."

My lips worked into a small smile as I took the jar from him. "I don't know."

"You don't know?" He flashed me a skeptical look.

"Yeah. I don't know what's going on in my head right now," I said as I put the jar to my lips. I downed a large gulp, not caring what flavor it was. My throat burned as the white lightning slipped down. The apple pie had burned, but this crap felt like lava.

"Whoa, take it easy," Eli laughed. "Maybe I should've warned you it wasn't flavored. No apple pie this time, just straight up Southern moonshine." He took the jar from me and put it to his lips. When he took a swig, I noticed his eyes water. "Whew, that crap is strong."

"Yeah, I can't feel my tongue and I think my throat might actually be on fire." Each breath seemed to flame it.

Eli agreed and then we lapsed into silence. My eyes zeroed in on the orange flames licking the inside of the barrel.

"I can't believe we found her," Eli whispered after some time had passed. "But what I really can't believe is that she was stuck in a damn cage like an animal."

"I'm sure that's how Drew thinks of us," I said unable to keep the disgust I felt toward him from leaking into my words. "I'm upset Glenn wasn't there, though. I feel like we let him down."

"We didn't let him down," Eli insisted. His warm gaze drifted over my face. "We're closer to finding him now than we were before."

"How do you figure that?"

"We rescued Violet. She has to know something."

I pulled the sleeves of his sweater over my hands. "Yeah, but who knows when we'll be able to ask her anything about it. She's passed out and I'm sure she'll be shaken when she does wake."

"She'll come to soon. Of course, she'll be shaken, but she'll talk. I'm sure of it."

I wished I could be as calm and collected about all of this as he was, but I couldn't. I felt like we'd let Glenn down from the very beginning. I didn't see how we could be any closer to finding him than we were before.

"We already know he wasn't at Drew's," Eli said pulling me from my thoughts. "We have the other brother's address. All we need to do is check his place."

"And what if Glenn's not there? What then?"

"We'll figure something out." Eli reached for my hand. I

slipped it free from the sleeve of his sweater and let him intertwine his fingers with mine. His warm touch was like a sedative. One that was instantaneous and I knew would end up being highly addictive. "We're going to find him, Mina. We'll bring Glenn home like we did Violet, even if it means taking down the other brother and whoever the hell is in charge of this whole thing along the way."

I nodded, agreeing with him, because deep down I knew this wasn't a situation I could let my emotions get the best of me in. I could only let them fuel me.

Our pack was being hunted, and I needed to find out why and who was running the show.

I leaned back in my chair and gazed up at the sliver of a moon hung low in the night sky knowing whatever it took I'd find the answers to both questions...even if it killed me.

THANK YOU

Thank you for reading *Moon Hunted*, I hope you enjoyed it! Please consider leaving an honest review at your point of purchase. Reviews help me in so many ways!

If you would like to know when my next novel is available, you can sign up for my newsletter here:
https://jennifersnyderbooks.com/want-the-latest/
Also, feel free to reach out and tell me your thoughts about the novel. I'd love to hear from you!
Email me at: jennifersnyder04@gmail.com

To see a complete up-to-date list of my novels, please take a moment to visit this page:
http://jennifersnyderbooks.com/book-list/

MINA'S STORY CONTINUES IN...

MOON SEVERED

Mirror Lake Wolves - Book Three

AVAILABLE NOW!

Sometimes admitting defeat is the only option...

Mina thought her questions would be answered once Violet woke. Instead, she learned Violet doesn't know any more than she does about who's behind the pack member disappearances. However, there is something wrong with Violet. Her werewolf healing should have kicked in days ago, but it hasn't.

Continuing the search for answers is the only option Mina sees. Too bad the alpha has given Eli and Mina a chaperone who's hell-bent on making sure their every move is one of caution.

While slow and steady might win the race, it hinders the discovery of a missing pack member and leaves the newly formed trio with only one option: Mina giving herself over to the vampire in charge as a prisoner.

Return to the world of werewolves and mystery in book three of the Mirror Lake Wolves series and get ready for more action and suspense!

Please Keep Reading for a sneak peek...

ONE

Two days passed before Violet woke. Three before Drew's body was found. Alec had been the one to tell me he'd been found dead, but even if he hadn't I would've heard about it anyway. Rumors flew around town like wildfire, spreading with each person's heated breath.

Mirror Lake hadn't seen something so *tragic* in years. At least not among the humans. The supernaturals? We were used to it.

Even so, it still shook me up. Maybe it was because of everything I knew firsthand surrounding Drew's death, or maybe it was because Shane had found him. As much as I didn't care for Shane, finding someone you loved dead wasn't something I would wish on anyone. Not even someone who was more foe than friend. I could only imagine how the memory would tarnish all others of that person. How it would haunt him for the rest of his life.

No one deserved that. Not even Shane.

I sent Becca a message telling her I was sorry about

Shane's brother. It seemed like the thing to do. Silence felt as though it would imply guilt, and I didn't need any more than what I already harbored.

The news of Violet waking had been darkened by Drew's discovery, causing my emotions to give me whiplash. Tension had melted away as gratitude slipped in only to be eaten to bits of nothing when I got the text from Alec telling me Shane had found his brother dead.

The image of Eli snapping Drew's neck had flashed through my mind on repeat since. The memory more vulgar and violent than the actual act.

Apparently, guilt could do that to a memory.

They found him. If we just lie low this will all die down soon. Remember he'd already hurt Violet. He planned to hurt you next. And who knows how many more members of our pack he would have hurt if I hadn't stopped him.

The text was from Eli. It came through as I stared at Alec's announcement of Drew's death. My face scrunched up as a lump built in the back of my throat. The image of Eli snapping Drew's neck shifted to Violet in the cage. Her mangled ankle. Her bruised and marred skin. I remembered how I'd thought she was dead, but how it turned out Drew had drugged her. Anger lapped at my insides.

Then I remembered Drew was dead, which meant the threat he placed on our pack had died along with him.

As sick as it might seem, a small sense of comfort slithered through my veins at the thought.

Until Shane entered my mind.

My heart kicked into overdrive as I wondered what went

through his head. Had he thought of the pack? Did he think one of us had killed Drew in retaliation for what he'd done? Did he think it was me?

Don't beat yourself up over this, Mina. We only did what had to be done. For the pack.

I reread Eli's last message, knowing he was right. Drew had to die for the safety of the pack. He wasn't one who could have been silenced by the fear of what we were or what we could do to him, because he already knew and he wasn't afraid. What he'd been doing proved it.

My mind drifted back to Shane.

Would we be able to scare him into submission so he left us alone? Or would drastic measures have to be taken with him too? I forced the thought away. I couldn't think about it. Yeah, I didn't like the guy, but that didn't mean I wanted him to die. He was young. Younger than his brother who should've known better.

My mind took me back to the night Eli and I hid in the woods, the night we overheard the conversation between Shane and Drew about their plan. Shane hadn't seemed as confident as his brother about what they were doing. He'd seemed scared. Or maybe somewhere deep inside him there were actual morals and what Drew was doing crossed them. If I was wrong, then fear would be our best motivator when it came to him. Especially now that we'd killed his brother.

My thumbs tapped across the screen of my cell as I replied to Eli's text.

I'm not beating myself up. I was there. I know it had to be done. - Mina

There was truth in my words but also lies. Even as I read

the text again, I couldn't distinguish which was which. There was a good chance Eli wouldn't be able to either.

What time do you want to visit Violet? - Mina

I asked for a swift change of subject. I needed to think of something else.

It had been a solid day since Violet woke. Gran had insisted we give her time before we bombarded her with questions about what happened.

Now. Let's go.

The breath I'd been holding expelled from my lungs. Thank goodness he wanted to go now. I didn't think I could wait another second. I wanted to know everything Violet knew. I needed to. Information was the only thing that was going to keep me sane. It was the only thing that could act as kryptonite to the guilt I felt surrounding Drew's death.

I'll meet you there. – Mina

I shoved my cell into the back pocket of my shorts and swiped a hair tie from my dresser. The desire to look into the mirror was too much of a draw to resist. As I piled my mop of long hair on top of my head, I cast a quick glance at myself. My eyes were darker than usual. Worry lines creased the area between my brows and forced my lips into a thin line.

I was the walking definition of guilt.

Inhaling a deep breath, I forced my face to relax. The tension in my shoulders eased as the worry lines between my brows faded. My eyes didn't brighten, but hopefully no one would notice.

Another text came through on my cell. The soft chime of it startled me enough to allow the mask I was building to fall away.

No need. I'm at your front door.

Relief trickled through me. Maybe it was wrong, but Eli's presence felt like a sedative to my frazzled nerves. Thankfully because I had been about to raid Gran's herbal pantry for something to help chill me out. Knowing me, I'd botch it and place myself in a coma. Herbs weren't my forte.

Guess Eli was good for something.

That was an unnecessary jab; Eli was good for many things. But I was just now realizing this.

I shoved my cell in my pocket. A whimper at my feet caught my attention. It was Gracie's little fur ball. His large brown eyes got me, and I bent to scoop him up. Even though I'd never admit it to anyone, I was grateful for the little guy. It was nice to have someone around who didn't talk, didn't drink alcohol, and didn't expect anything from me other than to show a little affection from time to time.

"Don't worry, little buddy. She'll be home soon," I told Winston as I scratched behind his ear while hugging him to my chest. "I promise."

Gracie had spent a lot of time at Callie's lately. I understood. Callie was her best friend, and her family was going through a lot. Gran had agreed Gracie could stay with Callie for moral support through today. After today she'd have to come home so Violet's family could spend uninterrupted time with her. Gracie understood. She was a good kid. A smart one. At thirteen, she was wise beyond her years. In fact, it hadn't taken her long to figure out something horrible had happened to Violet. She knew the story of her getting lost in the woods during a run alone wasn't the truth. There was no doubt in my mind Eli and me coming over today to talk to Violet would solidify that. Gracie would have questions, ones

I wouldn't be able to answer. Unless Eli said I could fill her in. Pack law had been in place regarding the situation since the beginning.

I placed Winston in his crate. His high-pitched, yippy bark echoed through our room. I hated locking him up. It reminded me too much of how we'd found Violet. Leaving Winston like this seemed cruel, but it was for the best. There was no telling what he would chew up or piss all over while we were all gone.

"It's okay. Gracie will be home soon. Chill out, little buddy. You won't be in there forever," I said as I pulled the striped beach towel over his crate so he couldn't see anymore.

It didn't help. In fact, it only pissed him off more. His bark became louder, and he scratched at the floor of his cage aggressively. My heart broke for him. Sometime over the last week, I'd grown to care for him. He was cute. There was no denying it. He also wasn't as much work as I'd thought he would be. He had a good temperament, and he listened decently well for his age.

I backed away from the cage and headed down the hall toward the front door. Eli was waiting. Even if he hadn't told me he was at my front door, I would have known.

I could feel him.

I opened the front door and stepped down the stairs. Eli was leaning against my car, waiting on me. He was dressed in a pair of gray cargo shorts and a thin ribbed white tank top. It seemed to be his signature look lately. I didn't mind. It showcased his muscles.

"Hey," he said. "Sounds like someone misses you." The corners of his lips quirked into a ghost of a smile. It was a jab at me. He knew I didn't like dogs, but what he didn't know was that this one had wormed his way into my heart somehow.

"He doesn't miss me," I muttered. Gravel crunched beneath my sandals as I walked past him toward the Marshalls' trailer. "He's pissed I locked him in his crate."

Eli caught up to me and matched his pace to mine. "Keep telling yourself that and maybe you'll believe it."

I rolled my eyes.

When we were halfway to Violet's, I risked a glance at Eli. His brows were pinched together in deep thought as he chewed the inside of his cheek. Was he nervous to talk to Violet? Was he worried she wouldn't have any new information?

His eyes shifted to mine, catching me staring. I blinked and looked away.

"Do you think she'll remember anything?" I asked. I had to say something. The silence between us was deafening.

"I hope so."

"What are you hoping she'll remember?" I asked as we neared the cinderblock steps that led to her front door. The steps were the only thing that made the Marshalls' place look temporary. Everything else about it seemed permanent. It was well cared for. In fact, it was one of the nicer trailers in the park. Navy blue shutters that matched the color of the front door hung beside all the windows. Mrs. Marshall had a beautiful raised flower bed that ran along the length of the front. Each spring she planted flowers in various colors. I asked her once why she didn't buy perennials knowing it would save her a lot of work, time, and money. She told me planting them again every year satisfied her need for change.

She could change the color. She could change the height of the plants. She liked that.

"I hope she remembers something about where Drew took Glenn. I hope she can give us more information on who's running this thing." His professional tone irked me. He was no longer just Eli. In the span of a few steps, he'd somehow switched to being the alpha's son on a mission.

I started up the cinderblock stairs that led to the Marshalls' front door and knocked.

Gracie stepped to the screen door and motioned for me to step inside. She looked upset. "Violet is in the back."

What was she upset about? Shouldn't she be happy?

Callie caught my eye when I stepped inside. She was on the couch with her legs tucked beneath her. She looked worse than Gracie. What was wrong? Why weren't they happy Violet was finally awake? Had something happened?

I started for the hall. The air was thick and charged with energy. Something was wrong. I could feel it as I inched toward the bedroom at the end.

"Something isn't right," Eli said, confirming my fear. "The energy here is too frantic."

"I know." I nodded in agreement.

The sharp scent of herbs lingered in the air near the door. Gran was inside, working her magic. I knew she was here checking on Violet, but I had no idea she'd be doing any sort of healing for her. Honestly, I thought we were beyond that. Apparently, we weren't.

"The lavender should help, but I think the tea will help even more." Gran's whispered words had my feet faltering. "She should be okay. We have to remember, she suffered a traumatic experience. In situations like this, it's not uncommon for abilities to behave this way."

To behave what way? Was Violet okay?

My mind raced with questions as I picked apart Gran's tone.

She was worried. About Violet.

Why?

TWO

I could count on one hand how many times in my life I'd heard Gran sound as worried as she did now. Most of them were in relation to my dad and his excessive drinking, his disability, and his broken heart over my mom leaving us. Never had I heard her sound so heart stricken about someone else in the pack.

The ajar door to Violet's bedroom swung open, and Gran stepped out. Her eyes locked with mine, and I saw exactly how worried she was for Violet before she could put up her walls.

"Mina," she breathed as her hand flew to her chest. "You startled me. I didn't know the two of you were here yet."

"We just got here. We wanted to visit Violet." The words slipped from my mouth before any question surging through my mind could.

Gran closed the door behind her. "I'm not sure Violet is up for visitors today."

"We have questions about what happened, about the

abduction," Eli insisted from where he stood behind me. His chest brushed against me as he moved closer.

"I don't think that's a good idea. She needs more time to recover." Gran folded her arms over her chest and flashed us a stern look, one I knew well. It meant there would be no negotiating with her. She'd made up her mind. No one was visiting Violet today to ask her any questions about what happened.

"This is pack business, and I'm sorry, but you don't have a say in the matter." Eli's voice was filled with authority. It had goose bumps prickling across my skin.

Gran unfolded her arms. Her chin lifted, and for a moment, I thought she was going to tell Eli where he could go for using that tone with her, but she didn't. Instead she stepped aside and swung the door open for us without a word.

"Thank you," Eli said as he squeezed past both of us and into Violet's room.

"Gran, I—"

"Don't." She held up a hand to stop my flow of words. "I don't need any apology from you. I don't need excuses or reasoning. I've told you Violet isn't up to taking visitors today. She's not well, but you've insisted on carrying out whatever pack business you're on. I'll be at home, making a few tinctures that hopefully will help heal Violet's mind, body, and soul sometime soon."

Gran started down the hall without another word. I remained mute and frozen. Never had I seen her so upset with me before. When she was out of sight, I stepped into Violet's room. No matter how much Gran wanted me not to bother Violet today, we needed to. I had questions only she could answer.

Violet sat on her bed. Her foot was propped up on a stack of pillows, and there was a goopy paste the color of baby poop smeared over her ankle. The aroma of herbs hung heavily in the air, but I couldn't distinguish one from the other to determine what Gran had used. A steaming mug of tea was clasp between Violet's hands as she gingerly sipped its contents. Silver jewelry adorned each of her fingers as well as her wrists. She reminded me of a boho princess. My gaze traveled up her arms. The bruises there had barely faded. Why? Was her werewolf healing not working? From the looks of her, it didn't seem as though it was. She should have been healed by now, but she wasn't.

This couldn't be good.

"Hello, Mina. It's nice of you to stop by," Mrs. Marshall said as I stepped farther into the room. "I don't think I'll ever be able to thank you enough for helping to bring my little girl home."

"You're welcome," I said with a small smile as I moved my attention from Violet to Mrs. Marshall. The woman didn't look as though she'd slept in days. One would think she'd be sleeping better now that her daughter was home safe and sound; however, that didn't seem to be the case. "I'm glad I was able to help."

"I know this is a difficult time, and were this situation any less grave or severe I would give it more time before asking Violet questions, but unfortunately we don't have that luxury," Eli said in a soft, soothing voice.

Even though there was a part of me that didn't appreciate the way he cut straight to it, I knew it was probably for the best. We needed information, and we needed it fast if we were going find Glenn or figure out who was behind all of this. I hoped Violet had heard a name during her time with Drew. Preferably of the one running the show.

"I know." Mrs. Marshall nodded.

Eli shifted his attention to Violet. "Is there anything you can tell me about your time spent with the guy who abducted you?"

Violet sipped her tea. Her glassy eyes stared at the thin blanket spread across the upper portion of her legs. What had Gran given her? A sedative for anxiety? I knew she'd spoken since waking. Gracie said when she finally woke she'd babbled about all sorts of stuff. None of it had made sense, but at least we knew she could speak still.

"Anything at all. It doesn't matter if it's small or seemingly insignificant. Any information you can give would be better than nothing," Eli pressed.

Violet remained unresponsive.

My skin tingled as the silence dragged on. Something was wrong with her. Shock? Or something worse? Had whatever Drew did to her broken her in some way? Or was this because of the drug he'd given her?

I stepped to where Eli stood and placed a hand on his shoulder, wanting him to step back and let me have a shot. He gave me some space, and I positioned myself on the edge of her bed. My hand reached out to cover hers. She was cold to the touch.

"I know what you went through was traumatic, but I want you to know the guy who did this can't hurt you anymore. Eli and I made sure of that the night we rescued you." My voice was soft as I leaned forward. I knew she needed to hear my words. Hell, her mom probably needed to hear them too. I hoped my words assuaged her fear. "You're safe. He can't hurt you anymore." I repeated it because it felt necessary.

Violet blinked and her fingers twitched, clinking a couple rings against her mug. I assumed she was going to take another sip of tea, but instead, she shifted to look me in the eye. Her wide eyes glistened with unshed tears as her lips quivered.

My heart broke for her.

"It's okay," I whispered as I held her stare. "You're home now. With your family. With your pack."

"Mina is right. This is a safe place," Eli insisted as he crouched down beside me. His hand gripped the edge of her bed, and my body became acutely aware of the mere inches separating my knee from the tips of his fingers. "Is there anything you can remember from that night we might be able to use to figure out who the person in charge was?"

Whispered words flowed past Violet's lips. I could barely make out what she'd said, but when I focused hard enough, her words made my heart stop.

"He wanted you," Violet repeated. "Not me. It wasn't supposed to be me. It was supposed to be you."

I knew this, but it still didn't lessen the blow that came with hearing her words out loud. Of course Drew had wanted me. That was why Shane had been so smug that night. He thought it would be the last time he ever had to lay eyes on me.

"I saw him watching you. Pure evil in his eyes. He hates what we are. He hates us. I didn't have to hear him say the words to know. I could feel it in the air around him. Hatred is a strong emotion when it's deeply rooted inside a person," Violet muttered as she placed the teacup to her lips. She took a small sip as the rest of us waited for her to continue. Her gaze drifted to me before she spoke again. "I should've listened to you. When I saw you in the woods I should have headed home, but I didn't."

"You were there?" Mrs. Marshall demanded. She'd remained silent until now, but I didn't blame her for speaking up. "You saw her in the woods, running alone and shifted? You told her to go home? Why didn't you say anything to me or my husband? To Callie?"

I didn't know what to say. Awful didn't do justice to describe how I felt.

"She was told not to," Eli said. His words were firm but not harsh. I shifted to glance at him, wanting to thank him for sticking up for me, but his gaze was locked on Violet. "Do you know why you were taken instead of Mina? Did he say?"

"I was weaker," she said matter-of-factly. I was surprised by how easily the words rolled off her tongue. "Mina is strong. She's a fighter. The guy who abducted me knew this. He brought two tranquilizers for her. He only had to use one on me..."

I wanted to tell her she wasn't weak, that the other tranquilizer had been used on Tate, but Eli flashed me a look that told me I should be quiet.

"Did he tell you what he intended to do with you?" Eli asked. I knew he was only asking to keep her talking, but I hated the way he'd worded the question.

When Violet's eyes lifted to find mine again, anger flared within their color. The air seemed to grow thick as it became charged with her rage.

"He was going to sell me," Violet insisted, her eyes never wavering from mine. "But he was going to do much worse to you. He watched you pretend to be normal, human, with his brother's friend, and he didn't like it."

Eli tensed beside me as a shiver slipped up my spine. I hadn't realized Drew held such hatred for me. Was that how Shane felt too?

Deep down, I knew the answer.

I forced my thoughts away. Drew was dead, and Shane didn't matter right now. Violet did. We needed to figure out who was behind all of this. They needed to be stopped.

"Do you know who he planned to sell you to?" Eli asked, keeping us on track with gaining new information. "Did you hear anything pertaining to the person in charge?"

Violet took a sip from her tea. Her eyes glassed over again, and for a second time I wondered what herbs Gran had used in her drink. Whatever it was it must have been something good, because each time she took a sip, she looked as though she were high on something.

"No. I don't know who he wanted to sell me to," Violet insisted. "But I think there was more than one person involved."

"What do you mean? Was he talking to more than one person on the phone? Or did more than one person stop by his house while you were being held there?" Eli asked.

Violet shook her head. "No. It was something he said. It sounded like he was double-crossing someone. He mentioned being afraid to have me at his place for long because they might find out. I can't remember much. The tranquilizer he gave me was strong, but I know he said something along those lines when he left a message with someone on the phone."

"There had to be a middleman to the whole operation then," I said. "That must be who Drew was talking to."

My mind raced with how big this situation might be. Eli and I might have bitten off more than we could chew.

"I never heard him say any names or places, though." Violet shifted around on her bed. She winced from the movement, and I was reminded again that she wasn't healing properly.

After I left here I planned to head home and talk with Gran. I wanted to know more about how Violet was doing health wise.

"I'm sorry but I don't know anything more," Violet insisted.

"Okay. If you think of anything, please let us know," Eli said as he stood.

It didn't go unnoticed the way he'd said *us* instead of *me*. We were in this together. I was glad he'd realized not including me was a deal breaker. I needed to see this all play out. I needed to know who was running it. I needed to help find Glenn.

"I will," Violet insisted before she took another sip of tea.

"I'll see you out," Mrs. Marshall said as she motioned us toward the door. We stepped into the hallway, and she closed the door behind us. When she spun around to face us, a look of worry pinched her features. "Is the person who did this to my little girl really no longer a threat?" she whispered.

I should've known the question would come. It was one any mother would think to ask, but still I hadn't been prepared for it. My tongue was like sandpaper against the roof of my mouth as I thought of how to answer.

"Yes, he truly is no longer a threat," Eli answered for me.

Mrs. Marshall's eyes zeroed in on him. A wild look flared within them that made unease prickle along my skin. "Did that dead Hopkins boy they found have anything to do with this?"

I couldn't breathe. I should've known people in the pack would piece it together on their own. Drew's death had been ruled an accident, which was exactly what we'd staged, but that didn't mean everyone would believe it. Especially not when one of our own had been rescued days before someone in town turned up dead.

"I'm not at liberty to say," Eli insisted. "Pack business. I'm sorry."

Mrs. Marshall soaked in Eli's reply. Her face shifted through a handful of emotions before settling on one—displeasure. Eli's answer hadn't been satisfying enough for her. She wanted a person to blame. A face and name. I understood, but I also felt it was better she didn't know. Knowing the one responsible had been taken care of, that he was no longer a threat, should be enough to satisfy her.

For anyone normal it would have been, but Mrs. Marshall was different. She was a werewolf, and just like the others in the trailer park, when one of our own had been hurt, we wanted to hunt down the person responsible and take justice into our own hands.

Eli started down the hall and I followed.

Gracie was on the couch beside Callie when we stepped into the living room of their single wide trailer. Her eyes flicked to me. I could see questions for me building in them. She wanted to know if I knew what was wrong with Violet. She wanted to know if she was right in thinking something was wrong. I chewed my bottom lip and held her stare.

Maybe it would be enough to get my answer across to her without using words.

Something was definitely wrong with Violet. She wasn't healing like she should, and I wasn't one hundred percent sure the glassy look in her eyes was all Gran's tea either.

Violet looked lost. Broken.

I needed to speak with Gran. I needed to know what her thoughts were on this. Mainly because a part of me still felt responsible for what happened to Violet. Maybe a part of me always would.

AVAILABLE NOW!

ABOUT THE AUTHOR

Jennifer Snyder lives in North Carolina where she spends most of her time writing New Adult and Young Adult Fiction, reading, and struggling to stay on top of housework. She is a tea lover with an obsession for Post-it notes and smooth writing pens. Jennifer lives with her husband and two children, who endure listening to songs that spur inspiration on repeat and tolerate her love for all paranormal, teenage-targeted TV shows.

To get an email whenever Jennifer releases a new title, sign up for her newsletter at https://jennifersnyderbooks.com/want-the-latest/. It's full of fun and freebies sent right to your inbox!

Find Jennifer Online!

jennifersnyderbooks.com/
jennifersnyder04@gmail.com

31372556R00128

Made in the USA
Middletown, DE
31 December 2018